Knot Just A Wish: Part One

Maren Marlowe

Author Maren Marlowe

Contents

Dedication

To younger me and the endless years I spent alone as an orphan collecting constellations of glow-in-the-dark stars, hoping someday my dreams and wishes would come true.

May love find us and loneliness lose us.

Anytime you need a safe space to call home for a little while, Mountain Glow Hot Springs Resort is here waiting for you with so much love.

Welcome to cozy Omegaverse!

Welcome to Omegaverse!

Each Omegaverse may be unique to its author. However, there are generally core ideas and elements that remain the same. Omegaverse is (loosely) an alternate world where humans are descendants of wolves. This means that biology and societal structures are different to the world you and I live in.

Here is an introduction into my Omegaverse universe...

Everyone born into an Omegaverse later show signs of a 'Designation', typically during early teen years. This means: Alpha, Beta, Omega designations.

What are Alphas?

Alphas are often associated with strength, leadership, protectiveness, etc. They're larger in stature than other designations and tend to naturally lean into forming 'Packs'. Some Alphas, while a little more rare, are inherently born with a knowing/well of deeper power that inclines them to be Pack Leads. This essentially means they are the leader and head of the pack/household.

Speaking in biological and physiological terms, Alphas also have what is referred to as a 'Knot' at the base of their penis. During sex, the knot inflates and 'locks' the Alpha and their Omega together.

It's believed that in prior years, before evolution, this was to ensure a higher rate of pregnancy. Alphas may occasionally use their 'Bark', which utilizes the natural inherent power they hold to control and command lesser designations (especially Omegas).

What are Betas?

Betas are essentially 'standard' humans as you and I are in our current reality. They are the backbone and majority of society often keeping the status-quo between the two other designations.

What are Omegas?

Omegas are often associated with being the more gentle, intuitive, submissive, and nurturing designation. They tend to thrive on physical touch, such as cuddling, and instinctively long to find their pack. Omegas experience what is referred to as a 'Heat'. This is an unavoidable period of time in which they're highly fertile and are driven by instinct and the urge to reproduce (this does NOT mean they will reproduce.) A Heat is also incredibly painful and may only be soothed by Alpha pheromones. A heat haze takes over, sometimes so severely the Omega may lose full consciousness. During this time, it is up to Alphas to care for and keep their Omega safe. Heat Leave is recognized by society and is a norm for packs to participate in (the period away from work to partake in a heat).

Omegas also tend to 'Nest' in an effort to self regulate and self soothe. This includes hiding and building safe, cozy, small spaces to seek refuge in. They're critical to an Omega's overall wellbeing. If an Omega finds themselves distressed, they release 'Whines'. Whines are a natural trigger for any Alpha (but especially Mates), to protect and comfort and them.

Details specific to this Omegaverse:

What's a Scent match?

A 'Scent Match' is essentially a soul mate that can only be experienced between Alphas and Omegas based on compatible signature scents. (Each A/B/O has a natural, identifiable, signature scent/pheromones).

In the Mount Fir's Landing Omegaverse, scent matches are 'Recognized' by their inner primals (inner omega/inner alpha). Typically, a 'Recognition Bond' will snap into place immediately. In situations where one or more of the matches do not feel safe in the other's presence, the Recognition may be slow to occur. The repercussions of this are nearly unknown.

What's a completed mating bond?

Alphas and Omegas sharing a 'Recognition Bond' are driven by instincts to form a 'Completed Bond'. This is a mystical, divine connection that bonds their souls on a deeply unique level we will never fully understand. The process is completed by the sharing and exchange of a claiming mark/bite. It may be different depending on the Omegaverse you're in, but, in Mount Fir's Landing, a beta may be bonded into a pack by receiving a claiming bite from both their Omega and Alpha. Once all members of a pack are bonded in, the connection is extended to the pack, allowing much stronger connections and insight to feeling the others' emotions.

What's a Prowler-Hold / 'Hold' Response?

A Prowler-Hold Response is also referred to as a 'Hold' or 'Guard' in my Omegaverse. The terms are used interchangeably. This is an event triggered in an Alpha when their Omega is in extreme distress or under severe threat, resulting in aggression and heightened protective/obsessive behavior.

What's a 'Drop'/ Regression?

A Regression is simply when an Omega's 'Primal' (or otherwise 'Inner Omega') is front and center, in control of their behavior.

A Drop is a couple of steps beyond a Regression. When an Omega is so overwhelmed, whether physically or emotionally, the body's response is to shut down to keep the Omega safe in horribly stressful or traumatic situations.

Note: Throughout the series, you will notice the word 'Primal'. In this Omegaverse, 'Primal' is used interchangeably with familiar terms such as 'Inner Omega' or 'Inner Alpha'.

With all that said... Enjoy!

1

Opaline

Current Day

Another sudden flash of lightning illuminates the night sky with terrifying, bright jagged streaks. For a quick, momentary second, the world around me is drenched in light, offering a much broader view of the storefronts lining the sidewalk I'm on. Various cutesy store names and window treatments stand out in stark relief. One of which I'm now leaning against, huddled under the building alcove's canopy.

Thunder follows like a bowling ball chasing its electric pins, stealing my breath with a gasp that's silent against the resounding booms, the heavy sound vibrating through my body. It rolls over the city with a deep growl and momentum that roots me to the spot, freezing my muscles in place. My inner omega, my primal, instinctively wants to submit and bare our throat to the storm, sensing the overwhelming natural power behind it. I release a frustrated growl of my own, fighting my instincts. It makes no logical sense, but I learned a long time ago that biology is a bitch sometimes.

Hands shaking from adrenaline and spikes of fear, I focus my attention back on gripping the umbrella that's currently fighting to emancipate itself from my grasp. Apparently, its unknown manufactured lineage must connect to the Gods with the way it's been screaming against my palms to fly home to the heavens.

Stepping out of the alcove, I'm hit with another gust of wind, peeking both ways. The streets are a ghost town, painted in the soft glow of streetlamps and occasional flashes of lightning from the storm overhead. The desertedness is a small blessing I happily accept. The lamps, every quarter block or so, offer enough guidance to find my way back to the unconventional shelter I now call home.

It could be worse. It could be worse. It could be fucking worse. The mantra loops in my head daily in a nearly obsessive compulsion. One of the many I'm leaning on as a pathetic anchor to keep me rooted in reality and, frankly, as a distraction to the gnawing void in my stomach and the ache of loneliness that fully bloomed weeks ago. No one understands the devastating effects of loneliness, especially for omegas and alphas. Some nights, I feel like I'm on the verge of slipping into some torturous brand of dissociation as everything around me becomes less and less real, leaning on this side of sinister. Nothing feels right anymore, nothing's familiar. It's just an unending sense of unease and wrongness that haunts me like a dark, sentient, and malicious cloud.

The urge to move nips at my heels. Tugging my lone suitcase behind me one-handed, I fight for balance, taking short breaks to keep the umbrella close to my chest as gusts of wind nearly take me to the ground. Rain lashes against my skin, soaking through the too-thin layers of my clothes, further slowing each step. The reality is simply that I couldn't chance leaving my most important possessions behind for my outing today. Hence, the awkward, oversized ball and chain working to make this as difficult as possible for me.

Six blocks later, I round the familiar corner into the dark alley. My muscles shake and scream from exhaustion, my stomach a hollow, begging pit. With an instant reprieve from the monstrous winds, I nearly fall into the worn brick wall closest to me as I step into the shadow, practically weightless in comparison. I look around and check behind me to make sure no one is watching me come through the alley, my ears honed to any rustle or sound indicating movement. As an unbonded omega, the need to be on a constant high alert and always aware of my surroundings isn't optional.

Omegas are the most sought-after designation between alphas, omegas, and betas. Being unbonded makes any target on my back that much bigger, and there are too many terrible people who would go to great depths to get their hands on me. Being auctioned off to an abusive alpha pack of gangster crime lords isn't on the top of my doodled *big-dreams* list, now long buried.

Picking up my suitcase in an effort to move quietly, I make my way quickly, leaning slightly from the weight, towards the very end of the alley, slipping deeper into the shadows. Had someone told me prior to all this that darkness lacking the glow of stars would become my comfort, I would have scoffed.

Rounding the building's far corner, the compounded weight of dread and anxiety slithers from my shoulders at the sight of my shelter and other box of belongings, still safe and untouched. I can't help but send a silent thank you to the skies for the generous canopy of trees over the area, too.

Before leaving the Omega Care Facilities, I was able to save a minuscule amount of cash, and one of the best things I did was buy cheap rope and this little blue tarp that's become my shelter. Desperate for food one night, I followed the greasy, garlicy scents of a kitchen and found this perfect nook of a space just big enough to sleep in with both my suitcase and second box. It's brick, just like the rest of the building, and a small square, trapping a vent that I assume leads directly to the kitchen. Maybe the vent from the grill? Either way, I'm grateful. The warm air pumps out nearly nonstop into the late hours of the night, and something so seemingly small has made my world a much more comfortable place, at least until I figure out what the hell to do next. Because this? This can't be my forever. It just can't.

I never expected, especially as an omega, that I'd ever be in this situation: homeless, alone, with no food, and seeking refuge in a makeshift back alleyway shelter. Statistically, no one could have expected this. A sense of shame washes over me at the thought of my mother seeing me in this situation. I still miss her, even after all this time since her passing. The urge to touch and tug on the necklace she gave me gnaws at my willpower to keep moving.

Crawling under the flapping edge of the tarp, I close my flimsy umbrella and tuck it next to the cardboard box of my things and tug my suitcase inside with me. A quick glance around tells me it's not as wet as it would be otherwise, thankfully. Positioning the standard-issued travel bag on its side, it acts as a weight, keeping the tarp even more in place, knocking out the wind entirely. The rain, not blocked by trees, drums steadily against the plastic above my head.

Unzipping the hard case of the luggage, I bite my bottom lip and exhale in relief to see Sparkles the fox, dry and smiling. This silly little stuffed animal has come to mean more to me than I could have ever thought possible. The weighted insert in her tummy soothes my inner omega; the aching, growing wound for touch and cuddles that only seems to get worse. Omegas aren't meant to be alone. By nature, we're the heart of packs, meant to be surrounded, held, and protected. Everything in me feels like unending chaos and loneliness now. I have literally no one. Sparkles is my only companion, my only constant I can count on.

Pulling out both of the blankets I took from the O.C. Facilities, I lay one down and cover myself with the other completely; only my eyes and nose peeking out, exposed to the damp air. A pathetic attempt at nesting. It's cramped with my belongings, leaving just enough room to sleep balled up. Snaking out my hand, I reach for the little fox, tucking her under the blanket with me. "Come here, cutie. You're ready for snuggles, aren't ya?" I ask. "Me too, little squish." Pressing her to my chest over my heart, I stroke her back and fluffy tail. The soft echoes of a purr vibrate my chest gently in an attempt to self-soothe. The rain is slowing a little, no longer any thunder or lightning dancing and painting the night sky, at least from what I can sense hidden and tucked away.

Softly, the barely-there voices of bar patrons and staff float through the vent. It's become a source of comfort. A temporary reprieve; a sense of not being entirely alone. If only it were true.

Closing my eyes, I let my purr, the white noise of the rain, and the waves of voices lull me to sleep.

2

Opaline

Twenty Two Days Ago

"But, I don't understand." I sit in the overly beige and wood-covered office, simultaneously feeling like the couch against my back and thighs is slowly swallowing me whole, and feeling like my head is about to float away, separating itself from the rest of my body like a balloon. I'm barely feeling tethered to reality, much less a scratchy couch.

"I know, dear. I'm sorry." Mrs. Lindal's voice is smooth and almost gentle. It could easily be misconstrued as kind. "This is out of my hands, though. I've done everything I can, and unfortunately, there's nothing to be done. There are protocols and operating procedures that the Facilities must follow. You've been here long enough to know this. We no longer have the resources to house an unbonded omega past the regulatory limit." Past the...regulatory limit? She nods, as if confirming her words, watching me with what would appear to be sympathy from a stranger's eye. It's the perfect amount of contrived pity. I know better. A decade of observing everyone and everything here allows these small insights.

Seconds pass in silence and I realize that's it then. I wait for her to further explain, to offer any sort of reassurance, but, no. Just a decision, sealed, stamped, and sent out, with no room for argument or my pleas bordering on breaking free.

I take a shaky inhale, digesting her words and their implications. The Omega Care Facility never felt like a real home, but it was safe, predictable, and offered much-needed structure. What certainty I ever felt within these walls is crumbling in a matter of seconds. The dream, the life we all plan for, is crumbling right there with them. The entire reason we're sent here as Omegas. It's being drenched in gasoline, and this wretched woman before me is throwing match after match down without a single care, completely unaffected by the weight of this news. Completely unaffected, as my entire life is upended.

It's unheard of to be twenty-eight and packless. Most residents, by and large, find their perfect matches within the first three to eight months. I've been here well over eight *years;* ten to be exact, and horrifically honest.

"So, what does that mean then? I just have to...leave?" A slight nod is her only response, coupled with a flat-lipped smile. "I...Mrs. Lindal, I have nowhere to go. I have no family or friends. What am I supposed to do? It's next to impossible to get a job in my designation without a guardian or pack to sign off on it. I have nowhere to stay. I just..." My breath catches as pressure starts to build behind my eyes, and I watch as she interrupts my clumsy outburst of thoughts. What kind of care facility suddenly shoves helpless omegas into a world they aren't prepared for? I can't wrap my head around this truly being my reality. I'd much prefer it were a sick, cruel joke at this point.

"Dear, I understand this seems frightening, but I assure you, a smart woman like yourself will be just fine. There are shelters...resources available for the transition."

"But–"

"You should be *grateful,* Opaline. Not only have you been blessed with the rarest, most desirable designation, but you've received a level of care that others would never be afforded. Especially those of different designations, and certainly not for this *long.* You should be thanking the O.C. Facilities for the support and care they've so generously provided until now." Her voice is clipped and intimidating, the weight of her barely leashed hate clinging to my chest like chilled syrup. The veiled mocking of my time here as an unbonded and the finality in her tone hits me just as hard, lungs fighting. I sit frozen as she straightens a stack of papers on her desk, the dismissal I'm all too familiar with, clear. Conversation over.

"Sandy will be in touch with further direction as you return to your quarters. We, at the Omega Care Facilities, wish you all the luck towards your future, Miss Williams."

Offering nothing more than a dazed nod, I push myself off the couch with shaky, weak arms, dizziness hitting as the weight on my chest stays in place, step after step out of the office. I swallow so many times in an effort to keep down the burn that's rising in my thickening throat that it's like my body suddenly forgets how to make the movement again and refuses to, causing me to nearly choke. Numbness extends through to my fingers as I walk towards my tiny room, thoughts too big for a physical body I can't entirely be sure belongs to me. To any onlooker, I'd be sure each unvoiced thought is visible, floating around me, existing independently. I can feel reality being pulled away from me in chunks.

A decade and still packless. Now homeless with no plan. What the hell am I going to do?

3

Opaline

Twenty One Days Ago

"Whisper your wishes to the night skies and know that somewhere, the stars and spirits are whispering back, my little gem."

For the first time I can recall from memory, I can't listen to my mother's advice. Her words replay in my head, and for the first time, they mean nothing. I don't have it in me to wish or dream, or even be hopeful. There's nothing left in me.

My reflection stares back through the square mirror hanging against a cream-colored, textured wall of my so-called room. Red, emotionally drained eyes and tear-stained cheeks capture my attention. It feels like a nightmare. The longer I stare at my own face, the more I become positive it's not actually mine that's looking back.

"Fuck." Squeezing my eyes tight, I turn around and take a shaky breath, palm to my chest. Again. And again.

Finally, I take a look around at the tiny room that's been my home. I didn't always stay in this room. When I first arrived, I had a cozy room assignment like every other omega at the Facility. Fluffy, soft comforters and pillows, a desk, small closet. A standard bedroom, as most would imagine. After three years and still showing no signs of offers from packs, they needed to open my room to another arriving omega. Which, at the time, didn't make sense. They had relocated me into this, which I suspect was actually a storage closet prior to my assignment. It wasn't big enough for a bed, desk, or closet like I had before. It had space enough for a small cot with a gel-like foam topper and...a trash can. But it was mine. That's all that had mattered to me. Because it was never supposed to be like this. It was never supposed to be a decade of my life wasting away inside these fucking neutral walls.

I was so sure, so naive, that I just needed a little more time. I just needed to be introduced to the right pack. The right alpha would find me, and everything would fall into place like it was supposed to. Like the dream, I prayed to the stars for over and over. Even on cloudy nights, and the nights locked away in this tiny windowless closet, I would continue the pathetic, nightly ritual and wish upon the small stars on my ceiling. A flush of embarrassment and shame and anger hit me so hard my chin wobbles, and another silent, soft round of tears leaves the corners of my eyes.

Foolish. I was so fucking foolish.

There, sitting on top of a short stack of clothes, lay a small, clear bag packed with the plastic glow-in-the-dark stars I've collected from childhood. The ones my mother helped me put up on my walls and ceiling, before she left me and the universe took her from me when I was just a teenage kid.

I'm suddenly so overwhelmed with too many emotions I can't even breathe. It's like every suppressed feeling is bombarding me like a tidal wave all at once. I can't do this. I can't. I'm so damn angry, I can feel it vibrating past my skin, filling every part of me, and I know it's too much, and I'm going to explode. Knowing I can't scream out loud, I ball my fists and release a primal silent yell, shaking from the effort and tension, imagining myself and my face as a fierce goddess on a battlefield heading straight into the fray with an unseen enemy.

Only *she's* surrounded by other women, other warriors by her side. I have nothing and no one.

Lightheaded and blood pounding in my skull, I clumsily attack the ridiculous excuse for personal belongings on my cot in front of me with grey stealing the edges of my vision. I put enough force to break something into the effort of throwing clothing onto the floor and against the walls, wishing it could make more noise. I want things crashing, and I want to fucking scream and let everyone know how I'm really feeling. I also know, no one actually gives a shit. The thought hurts just as deeply. I'm realizing they never did. Not once they started losing faith that I could ever gain them something; money and Facility donations from prospective wealthy packs, whatever.

I trip in my haste and fall on my hip, sideways, hitting the hard floor with a whine. The bag of stars I put all my faith in for so many fucking years mocks me at the version of myself I've become. This tear-stained and red-faced, pathetic version. Part of me pulls and pulls at my heart to not do this, to stop myself, but the rest of me, the cloud of emotion ruling me, draws my hand to the bag.

With a final squeeze, I throw it in the trash in the corner of the tiny room, just like the dreams I've now entirely given up on. I'm nothing but a broken omega.

No wish to the skies or spirits can save me.

4

Opaline

Twenty Days Ago

My feet shuffle quickly, carrying me down the gravel path leading away from the Omega Care Facility. Behind me, the huge, black metal gates close automatically, the clanging causing me to flinch. The guard on duty at the small shed by the entrance must be aware of my leaving since he let me through with no more than a short nod in my direction over the top of his newspaper in hand.

Obviously, since as of this morning, I was officially not their problem. It didn't matter that I was leaving alone or well before my scheduled ride for departure.

Part of me is tempted to look back. I guess, get a final look at the life I knew. I've been here before, though, and, looking back won't do any good. There won't be that moment, that second of closure or contentment. Instead, I focus my attention ahead.

Gripping the small cardboard box under one arm, I pull the suitcase they issued me behind with my free hand, its wheels bumping and rattling against the uneven rocks. After my tantrum, I had refolded everything and packed it neatly. Moreso for the sake of having something to do with my hands as my mind spiraled nowhere helpful. Fortunately, I guess, I don't have many belongings to haul behind me. What I do have, I desperately need. I've always held onto rations of snack bars and single-serve treats they gave us. I couldn't be more thankful for that now, knowing I have packaged food tucked away to take with me.

One of the security guards was supposed to walk me out to a ride they'd provide, dropping me off closer towards the city's center at a designated shelter. After tossing and turning, frantically trying to cultivate a realistic plan, I realized how dangerous a plan that actually was. The O.C. Facility couldn't promise my safety anymore.

Sandy had, as promised, come to my room and gone into a little more detail. The main reason of which, was my scheduled departure date and time, the security guard that'd be escorting me, and a piece of paper with a few local resources for housing and food since I'd be on my own. I huff in disbelief, replaying her words. I should have never put so much faith into the people around me, including my remaining father, who'd not answered any of their correspondence regarding my leaving the Facility. Not at all surprised. We haven't spoken or been in communication since he essentially sold me off to the Omega Care Facilities.

No, I couldn't utilize their recommended resources. An unbonded omega entering a building with little to no security, with no idea of the temperament and morals of its other current inhabitants? I wouldn't be able to sleep, constantly on alert for potential threats. Best case scenario, I had two meals a day and hopefully another cot to try to sleep on. Worst-case scenario, I would literally be kidnapped and sold, potentially raped, or trafficked. That alone was terrifying enough to make my decision for me to stay away. I'd rather chance it on my own.

The air is cooler than expected, but manageable with my jacket. Still, I pause and pull my hood up, cutting the dull wind. The sun's starting to rise, painting the sky in an unexpected, stunning orange glow. The beauty of it somehow makes the pain in my chest worse. The peaceful chirping of awakening birds and soft glow of the morning is a polar contrast to the turmoil killing me inside, eating at me slowly.

I'd spent my entire adult life being praised and told exactly what I was. It was drilled into each of us. I was an Omega. Special. Desired. Meant to be cherished, protected, and claimed by my pack of dreamy alphas. And now? I'm what? A facility burden, a castoff, a broken and useless omega. Worse, was the weight and truth of my being wholly unwanted.

A pathetic kitten growl of annoyance vibrates through me at the warm tears streaking my chilled cheeks. I'm sick of crying.

I'd been prepared for many things.

But I was never prepared for this.

Not for the first time in life, I feel what it is to be truly alone.

5

Opaline

Current Day

A rough, intrusive voice and what sounds like a screen door slamming startles me awake, my heart hammering through my upper body, panic hitting in a heavy wave. I listen, eyes wide, and get to my knees in case I need to defend myself or make a run for it with a small opening of time that might be presented.

The rain's stopped completely, and my senses home in on the details of my surroundings: rowdy people I can hear drunk on the street, most likely leaving the pub I'm camped out behind, cars, and a man much closer than I'd like. *Threat.*

Then the smell hits me...fuck. Some kind of a garlicy burger and greasy fries, if I had to guess. I squeeze my eyes shut and clinch my fists to stop the needy whimper that fights its way to the surface. My perpetually empty stomach desperately urges me to hunt the source and take it.

Focusing on keeping my body still to not make a sound, I hold and listen. A lighter's brought to life followed by a sharp metallic material snapping before a wave of nauseating smoke floats towards the end of the alley. It sounds like he's on the phone chatting quietly, or maybe just talking to himself. No judgment here. Hell, my best friend is a cotton and rice-filled stuffed animal.

I hear the same door slam open again, and a second man raising his voice about something someone else did, from the tidbits I can decipher. A murmured series of curses slips free from the smoker that sounds an awful lot like *'mother-fucking-god-damnit'* followed by a third, but slightly softer slam of the door...and then silence. I'm slipping past my suitcase and out from my tarp before I even have time to second-guess myself. This might be my only chance for real food, not from a dumpster or a wrapper, in weeks.

I stop at the end of the wall closest to me and peek around the corner, the cold brick wall rough under my palms. It's silent outside of the chatter past the alley, dark shadows creeping over the building walls, warring against the streetlamps flooding the opposite end towards the street. There, a white to-go box is sitting on the cement stairs at the bottom of the alcove of the back entrance to the bar. The light of the small, covered space reflects off the container like a sign from the universe, and holy music should be playing.

A quick sniff makes me stiffen, though. Alpha. More than one that I can scent. So the owners of the voices are both alphas, then. The scents of sweet chocolate-covered cherries and a lighter scent of worn leather linger. I crinkle my nose at that one. Anxiety rushes me, making me almost pause, but this is it; my only sure chance. The split decision to run and grab the container as quickly as possible beats any rational thought of creeping up silently and slowly to stealthily grab it.

Trying to be light on my feet, I race toward the steps, staying close to the wall. Less than ten feet away, the door slams open, light spilling out and coating everything with a glow. A huge, terrifying alpha steps down as I fall, scrambling to turn and run back. Small rocks scrape and nick my hands and knees, breathing heavy, my lungs overwhelmingly desperate for air, aware of this sudden threat. *No, no, no…no.*

"Stop." The command is gentle enough leaving his lips, but there's no denying he used his bark, my shaking body now frozen in place as a result. "Omega?" His face lifts slightly, like he's trying to get a read on my scent, walking down the remainder of the short series of steps.

A whine breaks free of my throat as tears cloud my vision and start to fall from the edges of my eyes. Images and visions of the worst outcomes jumble together, increasing the shake in my limbs.

"Hey…" he damn near whispers. "You're okay, little omega. *Shh, shh, shh.* You're okay. I'm not gonna hurt you." He steps closer to me, now just a few feet away. Shivers wrack my body, and I nearly start sobbing, his barked command still holding my inner omega in place. "Fuck. Sweet girl, you're okay. Here, get a sniff. I'm already bonded, little one. I have my own omega waitin' for me at home. 'Kay?" He slowly brings his wrist down, closer to me, and despite the part of me that just wants so badly to be able to run away, I take a small whiff and realize he's telling the truth. His signature scent has the tell-tale twist of being bonded and already claimed, his omega's scent clinging to him. He's also the chocolate-covered cherries I smelled.

"There, see? Come on up, you're okay." Reaching out his hand the rest of the way, he offers it to me to help me stand. I stare at it for several seconds, the huge size of it compared to mine, the rough patches of skin on his palms, and the thick plaid flannel ending at his wrist. Wiggling my nose towards his sleeve, I get another, deeper scent of lavender and whine again out of sheer relief. He is telling the truth. The light, lingering, lavender scent is all omega and washes over me with a calming wave, blending with his own cherries.

Lifting my shaking hand to his, he gently helps tug me up to standing and then steps back a few feet. "What're you doing out here at this time of night by yourself? It's not safe for omegas. Do you have alphas, little one?" His rough voice manages to come out soft, a drastic contrast to the gruff mountain of a man in front of me, now.

Getting a better look at him, he's older with greying hair and a big beard. His shoulders look like they're three times the width of mine. He's bonded, but that doesn't make him safe. My eyes must jump to the white to-go box behind him on the steps because he follows my path and looks back to me quickly, reading me and observing me.

I'm sure he sees it all now. The dirty clothes, the messy hair, dark circles under my eyes, and a continuous shake in my hands from hunger that won't go away. Slowly nodding, he reaches back and bends to pick up the container and opens it, showing me the food inside. A half-wrapped, shiny burger and a handful of french fries sit atop a square of red checkered tissue paper, untouched.

I'm not sure why this is the moment that does it, but everything in me wants to bleed out this horrible, desperate need that's not gone away since leaving the center. I feel my face crumple, a thick sob caught in my throat, as my knees nearly give out. "Hey, little one, you're okay. Here, take it. It's all yours and anything else you want, got it?" I blink the silver from my eyes and track the feeling of tears sliding down my cheeks, chin shaking, looking up at his mostly shadowed face. A gentle smile tilts his lips hidden by a bushy beard, and he reaches the food towards me, practically pushing it into my hands. "Yeah? It's all yours."

I give him a tiny nod and hesitantly reach for it, bringing it close to my chest. Eyes torn between watching him to make sure he doesn't move, and eating the food...the food wins and I reach for the burger and take a huge bite. The slight moan that I release should be embarrassing, but god, this fucking burger is the best thing I've tasted in so long, even before leaving the Facility. The foods they made us eat there were all omega-diet approved.

A deep chuckle makes me pause, and my eyes, which I didn't realize I had closed, snap open to see his arms crossed and a goofy smile sitting on his face, before he slowly sobers and looks me over again.

6

Opaline

"What's your name? Will you at least tell me that much?" He watches me, his face unreadable right now, but lifts a brow, waiting. I want to trust him, to believe him. I want to believe he's good, but, god, I'm exhausted, hungry, terrified, and honestly a little too close to completely hopeless. A strange alpha in a dark alley still has me ready to bolt if I need to.

I swallow the huge bite, setting the heavy burger back down in the container, holding it while mindful of its weight so it doesn't collapse. Clearing my throat, I offer him my very real name. I most definitely did not blurt out whatever came to me first. "S-Sparkles." The seconds of silence that stretch between us feel like hours as any semblance of comfort is killed. Heat rushes over my neck and up onto my cheeks and I pray he can't see it.

"Uh huh. I'll just bet... Family name?" He sucks on his top teeth, and it looks like he knows I'm fibbing. *God, Opaline... Sparkles was the best you could do?* I lower my head and keep eye contact with his boots before sneaking a quick peek at his face and slowly grabbing a couple of fries and shoving them in my mouth. Chewing slowly, I just shrug. A sizable snort practically echoes between the buildings on either side as he shifts a little, clearing a path to the door behind him. "Well, come on then, Princess Sparkles."

Giving him a curious look, I hold the container tighter, knees tense, ready to run.

"You wanna stay out in the cold, or you wanna come inside and bundle up in a warm booth while I fix ya some hot chocolate? Whatever the hell else ya want, too." God, the offer is too good to be true. A million ways this could go wrong start fighting for dominance in my mind's eye before I shake my head and shut the nasty, horrifying imagery down. Ultimately, my desperation wins. I consider and realize I'd be leaving all of my valuable items outside unattended. I doubt anyone knows I'm there, but I just can't risk it. I can't. It's my entire life summed up into six square feet. I glance at the end of the alley and back to the big alpha.

"My...umm. My stuff is back there, and I can't leave it." It somehow comes out as more of a question than a statement, but he seems to understand, nodding back to me.

"I'll get it. Come on then."

A squeaky omega growl vibrates my throat, sending me cowering and dropping to my knees in submission, dropping the food too. I can't believe I just growled at a fucking alpha. Part of me wonders if maybe I'd already started losing it the past few weeks, alone and mostly isolated. A whimper leaves me as I ball up, tense, waiting for his palm or his boot, something to punish me for growling at him. "I'm sorry. I'm sorry. I'm sorry."

"Hey, little one." He kneels close enough that I can actually feel the heat from his giant body. "Look at me, princess." A soft bark fuses with his words, and I look up, meeting his eyes. There's no anger, though. No. Something undoubtedly worse. "Look, little thing, I can see you're in a bad way. I know how easy it would be to run and hide, to not trust me, take the food, and go." He sighs. "But, I just ask that you give me a chance. Get some food in your tummy, something warm to cozy up with, and even put on the tv for ya. Trust my alpha to take care of you and to handle this. I promise, I would never hurt you or any omega. The most precious gift to our world. Yeah?"

I don't know what it is. Why I would so simply believe this stranger. This huge, scary alpha. But something deep in me is practically pushing me to fall forward and go along with it. Another vision of the worst that could happen flashes in front of me as I close my eyes: being kidnapped, taken advantage of, being *sold.*

The moment my eyes open again and meet his, I realize my inner omega, my primal, is telling me it's okay.

And I need to trust her, too.

The giant follows me, a few steps behind as I lead him towards my tiny home. Discreetly, I sneak quick peeks to follow his location and track any changes in body language.

Rounding the corner, it's oddly a small relief seeing my things. A guttural growl reverberates off nearby brick, making me jump and turn to face him. Losing my footing, I collapse into the rough wall, more than a little tense at the sound and its implications. "Shit." He forces a deep breath out, hands up in a display of surrender, neck slightly open to me in the ultimate show of safety. "Sorry, princess. You're okay. I just... fuck. This is where you've been sleeping? Living? For how fucking long?" He paces a few steps. "Right under my fucking nose and I didn't even realize it." He releases another short growl before stifling it, quickly getting a look at my face, my eyes wide and watching. "I keep fucking this up. Damn it to Hell. You're okay." He steps slowly towards my shelter as I track his movements. "You okay if I help you pack and carry your stuff inside?"

I'm shaking, trying to keep my chin from wobbling, reflecting my inner turmoil. Forcing even breaths, I focus on my inner primal again and the trust to follow her guidance. She trusts him, so I can, too. "Yes, please."

"You got it, pup."

7

Opaline

What feels like a few short minutes later, my new friend has me set up in a booth under a fuzzy dark blue blanket with a huge plate of fresh fries, a bubbly soda, hot chocolate, and chicken tenders in front of me as my own personal buffet. The bar/restaurant's now empty; all his staff officially gone for the night, the lights pleasantly low. There are rows of booth seating with cropped wooden dividing walls in between them, stools along the stretched bar top, and mirrors and bottles behind the bar itself. Everything is coated in a glossy shine that glitters under the low lighting. Surprisingly, it's very clean, in all aspects. There are pops of green and gold throughout that catch my eye, including the seating I'm currently in.

He steps out from behind the long, glossy bar, a remote in his hand that he sets down in front of me. I realize he turned one of the huge TVs above the rows and rows of alcohol on, a quiet and gentle murmur of background noise.

"May I?" He stands next to the booth I'm occupying with a hand stretched out as if asking my permission to sit.

"Um, yeah." Something registers with a nervous itch in my brain that I should probably start providing more than two-syllable answers to this man who's done so much for me tonight. Just a single night off the streets and being able to sleep on this cushioned booth bench would be enough to make me cry tears of joy. A blessed reprieve from the nightmare my life's turned into. To have a place to close my eyes, knowing I was safe... "Thank you. I.." I clear my throat a little. "I appreciate the help for tonight and all this food."

He eases down into the booth, grace not accompanying him, the table wobbling and nearly pressing into his stomach as he settles in. He's huge. Not out of shape, he very clearly still takes care of himself and has alpha genetics coded into his skin. I have to fight back a smile at the image of the giant alpha in the smaller booth, catching my soda as it tilts, before it falls. I must not do as good a job as I think I am in fighting it because his face relaxes, a smile mirroring my own. "You have a beautiful smile, little omega." For some reason, I find myself embarrassed at the nice compliment, ducking my head and picking up the sweet drink he gave me. The huge, chilled, red plastic cup nearly takes both hands to hold. The words, coming from him, feel like another new layer of comfort. I know it's not flirty or him making advances on me. It's more of what I imagine having a grandpa or real father would be like. A huge, terrifying, gentle giant of a grandpa.

"So, what's your name?" He talked a little while getting me settled inside about this being his bar, that's his pride and joy, and about his bonded omega and other packmates. But never his name.

"Rainbow." He responds with an overly straight, flat face, and I narrow my eyes playfully at him before a barking laugh spills out of him, bouncing off the walls, his stomach pushing into the table on each inhale. I can't help but duck my head and silently chuckle, too.

I guess I should give him something real of me. Sparkles was a little obvious.

Tucking my dirty hair behind my ears, I reach my hand over the table to shake his. "Opaline." His laugh dies down, and he places his hand in mine too gently to be a coincidence.

"Remi, little one. It's nice to meet you," he smiles.

We sit in silence for a while, outside of the TV quietly playing a show with a laugh-track, while I eat, Remi stealing a few fries here and there. Eventually, he catches my attention, asking and prodding, curious about the obvious. I was hoping I'd somehow get away without this conversation.

I manage to give a quick overview, keeping things light enough so he doesn't feel the weight of my trauma dumped onto him.

The laughter and voices from the television drift to the background as I fall deeper and deeper into my head. The fact that I'm sitting with a stranger in a bar, all of my belongings are packed and stuffed into a box and a suitcase, and I have no way to check in with anyone from the O.C.F. And it hits me too, that there's no one that I would even want to check in with, given the chance. I never really made true friends there, the entire ten years I was there. I started showing signs of my designation, albeit a little late, just before turning eighteen, and was quickly pushed and essentially sold by my father to the Omega Care Facilities. I haven't spoken to him since and have no desire to.

The fact that I still wasn't able to find a pack in so long probably speaks volumes about me as an omega. Omegas never age out of the Facility. It's unheard of. I have no family, no friends, no pack, no home, no bed, I have nothing. Not to mention, no real plan. The crushing weight of reality hits me, and I feel my face crumple, the numbness of hopelessness traded for anguish that's drowning me so soon again. I try to hide it, reaching for a napkin. Before I have the chance, a heavy arm settles on my shoulder, pulling me into a hard but pillowy side.

"Let it out, pup. Let it out. Not good to keep things bottled up for too long." He murmurs kind things, and that somehow makes it even worse, the tears coming harder. The simple fact that someone, another person, cares enough about me in this moment to feed and hug me and comfort me is overwhelming. A part of me just sees myself as so undeserving, an utter burden. I'm not the one who deserves this kind of treatment. Sobs roll through me until eventually, my tears dry up, and I'm overcome with a fresh layer of numbness and a fog of exhaustion. All the while, Remi strokes my shoulder and pats my back softly like people in movies do. Like my mom used to do. My inner omega preens at the physical touch, so contented to be hugged and cared for.

Pushing back from him, I dry my eyes, clear my throat, and apologize for ruining his night. God, I'm such a mess. He probably wanted to go home to his pack and his omega and snuggle in their nest. And here I am keeping him away, late into the night. And, he's going to smell like me, which is just going to make her upset with him, all just for trying to help a pathetic girl on the street.

"If you don't mind, would it be okay if I took this food in a to-go box with me? I don't want to eat it all now in one setting. I'd like to save what I can. If you have a cup you can part ways with, that would be incredible. I've been using the water spout around back. But having a cup would be a game-changer."

He looks like he's biting back words and finally nods slowly, resting his forearms on the table in front of him. "I think you should stay here tonight. It'd make me happy to know you had a warm, dry place to lay your head and sleep knowing you're safe." I start to argue, but the stern look he gives me makes me lose all train of thought, and I nod, agreeing, before actually realizing it. "Good. Now, I have a small throw pillow and another blanket in my office. I have a chair in there, too. You're welcome to nest out here in this booth or take the chair. Have your pick." I like the idea of having the TV to watch to fall asleep to. It's been so long, just the imagery is mesmerizing on the screen.

"I'd like to stay here if that's okay."

"You got it, little one. I'll take the recliner in the office then. Don't worry, all the doors are locked, and there's a nightmare of a security system in place thanks to my son and his pack. You're safe here, just focus on resting tonight. Yeah?"

"You're going to stay here? W-what about your omega and your pack?" I ask, mild panic seeping into my tone, confused and a little concerned for multiple reasons. Mostly having them mad at Remi for all of the decisions he's making tonight to help me. "But—"

He puts up a hand to stop me, getting out of the booth and standing to his full height. Jesus, he's got to be close to seven feet tall. "I just need to make a couple of quick calls before I call it a night. There's a bathroom down that hallway on the left if you'd like to clean up a bit. Should be a stack of towels in the storage closet in there, but I'll grab a softer one from my office and set it outside the bathroom door for ya. Take your time, no rush."

"That...that would be great. Thank you, Remi." The sincerity of my words chokes me a little, and I fight more god damn tears as the heat swells to my cheeks. I make a beeline for the hallway, towards the clearly marked, 'employees only' bathroom, more than a little excited for access to hot water to clean up with.

8

Calder

Black type bleeds and blurs in front of me, the letters floating and next to useless. I've spent the better part of an hour in bed, rereading the same few pages, words blending together, not taking root in my brain. Now, apparently, even the occasional word isn't even landing amongst my scattered thoughts. Releasing a huge sigh, I give up and half-heartedly toss my book down next to me, pulling a knee up and resting my forearm on it, my head against the soft headboard.

Fuck, I don't know what's under my skin tonight. This sudden restless energy. The last few hours, something's just felt...off. The last several weeks have, in fact. I'm not entirely sure it's something bad, but, it's enough to keep my attention drifting back to what the hell I'm feeling coursing under my skin. Chewing on my lip, my head keeps being pulled to the row of windows to the right, leading to my balcony. Curiosity forces me to stand and make my way outside, grabbing a throw blanket from the armchair nearby.

The wide expanse of mountains surrounding us greets me as I push open one of the doors, wrapping the blanket around my shoulders. The chill is a little shock to the system as it hits after leaving the warmth of my bed, but not terribly cold. We still have several months before the next season's change, bringing with it snow and cold. The sea of lights down in the valley glows and flickers, soft orange illuminating small outlines of buildings, houses, and shops in the town center. A little closer to the side, the Mountain Glow Hot Springs Resort sits against the walls of darkness. From here, I can just about make out where the Main Lodge is on the grounds.

My pack brothers and I own it, brought it back to life about seven years ago. I'm not sure any of us really expected it to be as successful as it's been. Hard work, resilience, and many long days and nights onsite made it a reality, though. I can't help but still feel pride looking back at all the dedication of my pack. I'm lucky.

Movement above me catches my eye, and I manage to catch a shooting star amidst specks of light spanning the full sky. The awe it inspires is instant, reminding me of the one I saw when we moved to the mountains, the first night in our home. Goosebumps spread like wildfire, lighting up my skin with electricity at the sight, just as my phone vibrates against my nightstand through the open door. Glancing, I see the screen lit up and look back towards the glittering expanse of stars, but it's no longer in sight.

I'm not sure who'd be calling this late, and I make quick strides to pick it up, seeing Remi's name on the bright screen. Panic seizes my chest at the thought that something might be wrong. I answer, bringing the phone to my ear, sitting on the side of my bed, and throw down the blanket that's suddenly a little suffocating. "Hey, Dad, everything okay?"

"Well..." He huffs out a breath, and I can't tell if it's a laugh or what. It does absolutely nothing to ease the grip of the vice around my ribs.

"Remi, what's going on? Why are you up this late? Is someone hurt?" I swallow deeply, fist clenching at my side.

"Hey, calm down, son. Everything's fine. There is nothing wrong. Your mom and other dads are fine, too. I'm sorry to be calling ya this late. But, it can't wait."

A breath whooshes out of me, my spine relaxing. "Alright, sorry. Overreaction. I just... I don't know. Something's up tonight. Just anxious, I guess." His hum on the other end doesn't answer my previous question, though. "So... what's going on? Shouldn't the bar be closed by now? Why are you awake?" His chuckle in response damn near makes my hackles rise. Why he's suddenly speechless.

"You uh, happen to have any jobs available there at the resort?" The new topic seems out of left field, and I wonder if Rem might have gotten his hands into his own hooch. The image has me fighting a snort, gripping the bridge of my nose.

"I mean, not really that I know of right now. Maybe before the busy season picks up here soon. I could talk to Jewel, though. Why, what's up?"

"Hmm, that's a shame. I just had something in mind. One second, Calder." A feather-light feminine voice murmurs on the other end of the phone, and a fucking shiver wracks my body that has nothing to do with the air flowing in from outside through the door I left open.

"Who the fuck was that?" I don't mean for my tone to sound accusatory by any means, but that's exactly how it comes across.

"Sleep tight, pup."

"Huh?" Pup? He hasn't called me that in years. What the fuck is happening? It hits me a second later that he must be calling the owner of the voice on the other end, pup. "Rem, can you please start using words in your vocabulary I know with certainty you can use? Who was that?"

The sound of a door shutting echoes over the line as he finally starts to fill me in.

By the time he's finished, my jaw aches from the sheer force behind the clench taking up its home in my mouth, my chest now tight for an entirely new reason. Fury rages against my skin.

9

Calder

"Hey man, wh—"An *oomph* slips from Sage as I practically tackle him coming around the corner into the kitchen. "Jesus, what's going on? You good?" His brows are furrowed as he looks me up and down, searching my face for some clue or inclination, and then at the floor where he's spilled his drink. He looks mussed, bare-chested in sleep pants, a mug of what I assume is hot tea in his hand. Seems he's struggled with sleep tonight, too.

"I'm going into the city," I practically bark out.

"The city? Right now? What, why?" he asks, dark brows pulling together like long-lost lovers.

I just shake my head in disbelief and more than a little residual anger. "Remi just called. Apparently, he found an unbonded omega sleeping under a fucking tarp behind his bar." My words come out with the shake and deep tenor of a growl I can't exactly hold back.

"What? An omega? By herself? Why... how? I mean—" I raise my palm to stop his train of thought. Another fifteen minutes and he'd catch up to where I am, still seething and baffled at the information. "Is she —err, he, they, okay?"

"I'm not sure, to be completely honest. He's got her fed and warm, sleeping in the bar for the night."

"The bar?" He sucks in a breath, chest rising with the movement, a hand running through his black hair, gripping the roots. "Fuck, I guess that's better than the alternative. Jesus christ. Is that where you're going? The pub?" He glances down at the keys in my hand. I nod in return once, confirming his thought.

"I'm coming with you." It's on the tip of my tongue to stop him, but why would I deny him, stop his alpha instincts from taking over exactly as mine have? "Give me two minutes to throw on clothes and shoes. Should we wake the others?" I watch his retreating back, steaming mug now forgotten on the kitchen island.

"No. Adrian's probably out doing stupid shit on his bike, and Everette is still at his silent retreat on the coast. I'm not exactly sure what the outcome of this will be just yet, anyway. I think for now the less Adrian knows...the better."

"Wanna text Rem and let him know we're close? He might've passed out in his office for a few hours of sleep." Although just the thought of that seems ridiculous with a distressed omega thirty feet away from him. I know I wouldn't be able to sleep. I guess I'd be doing the same as my dad was earlier...trying to feed her, put a roof over her head, and make sure she was safe.

"Yeah, I just did a few minutes ago. He's up. He's going to meet us outside, out front." He huffs as another chime sounds, another text coming through. "He wants us to stop for coffee." Irritation niggles in my chest, but I can't fault my dad. He's done so much and has unexpectedly been up for far too long. The few minutes it takes to swing by a cafe won't hurt, despite my brain's protest telling me we have to get there as soon as possible.

About fifteen minutes later, we're passing the skyline to the right of the massive highway we're cruising on. We're about another twenty out from the pub and have been driving for several hours. The sun is just barely starting to change the color of the sky from a dark blue to a lighter purple. The change is reflected on some of the glass buildings as we pass. It's crazy to see so many cranes sitting, half-built apartments and skyrises going up everywhere. Seven years ago, it didn't look like this. It was starting to get built up when we decided to head into the mountains to take on the resort, but nothing like this. It's beautiful. Every now and then, I start to miss living downtown, but, the older we get, I think we all agree the small town in the mountains we've made home feels right for us. A little slower paced, familiar faces, and we're surrounded by natural beauty, no matter where you look.

The mountains are healing. I swear by it. I used to take weekend drives, solo, when we used to live down here, into the hills, chasing that feeling it always elicited. The moment, coming over the same ridge in the highway that just opens up to a unbelievable massive expanse of snow-covered mountains. The feeling of pure hope, peace, and contentment would wash over me every damn time I crossed that point. I guess I should have known then that the mountains were meant to be home. Yeah, there's no doubt in my mind that there's magic and hidden energy alive around us, healing us on a deeper level.

Dad mentioned he had something in mind for the omega, but, he left it at that. Although it's easy to guess exactly what that plan is. Especially if he's asking me about available positions we have open at the resort. If we can offer her a safe place to call home, food, and maybe even a job to earn her own money? It's the least we can do. It's in our very nature, our DNA as alphas, to protect and provide for omegas. Even if we don't have any openings, we'll figure something out.

I can't help but jump to the idea that maybe some time in the mountains will help heal this woman, too. Everything in me, every part of my inner alpha, wants to race to do anything we can to help the poor girl. Omegas are precious. They're rare enough as it is. But, fuck, an unbonded omega living on the fucking streets? Unheard of and unacceptable. If I let myself sit with the feeling too long, an unknown rage boils to the surface each time.

There have to be resources and shelters, but the thought stops short almost immediately. Not only are they probably packed to capacity, but there's also no telling how safe they'd be for an unbonded or if she'd be targeted for too many unsavory reasons to count. God, she's probably terrified. Tension and nausea in my gut work their way north, thickening my throat to an uncomfortable degree.

No matter what, I'm not leaving here without a plan to help her.

10

Sage

Pulling through the main strip of the Old District, we'd passed the historical shops, bars, and other odds and ends places. Charming little neighborhood overall. Calder's pops had met us out front of his pub, trading hugs for the coffee we stopped and got for him, *and us, obviously.* He filled us in outside, on the omega's situation, and my heart about fucking jumped out of my chest of its own accord. She's not even my omega, and all I can think about is holding her and keeping her safe tucked under a pile of blankets and pillows, feeding her fries, since I know she likes those now. My alpha is riding me hard and I know without a doubt, Calder is damn near fighting his for control. He's always been more heavily swayed by his alpha, though. Not in a hold-on-to-your-shorts borderline feral sense like Adrian, but, he's our pack lead for a reason. Many reasons.

"Before we go inside, just take a breath and make sure you've got your primal under control, okay?" A *ppfff* sound nearly rips its way through my lips, but I manage to bite it back. If anyone needs to take a breath, it's Calder. I really don't think he even realizes how affected he is. "We don't want to scare her, with three big men suddenly surrounding her, you know?"

"I definitely know. Do you?" I push emphasis on the *'you'* and snicker a little at his annoyed expression. I quickly sober, though, remembering the entire reason we're here and having this conversation at all. I have no doubt in my mind that we can help her.

Rem went in a couple of minutes ago to just chat one-on-one with her, letting her know we're safe and who we are. I watch through the glass on the red front door as he walks towards us, opening it to usher us inside.

The lights are still a little low, but the morning light from the rising sun bathes everything close to the windows in a soft glow. Passing a few booths on the left, the bar top crawls the length of the space to our right. There are more tables and another row of booths to the far left, behind a dividing wall distinguishing the respective bar and restaurant spaces.

It's when we get about twenty feet away from the final booth that it fucking hits me; the scent knocking me damn near on my ass. It's intoxicating...wild honey, brown sugar, and a hint of something soft, sensual, and feminine.

My senses heighten to a staggering degree with one goal: to find the source. The signature scent calls to my primal in a way I've never come close to feeling. A flurry of tension and energy fighting to be expelled floods my muscles. It's an active battle to fight the fog creeping in at the edges of my homed vision. To fight the overwhelming urge to flip and push past everything in front of me, blocking me from...from... A silent, possessive growl vibrates my chest and throat. This isn't just an omega's signature scent calling to me or my inner alpha. This is designed *for* me. My body's tight, every muscle tense as my locked-down primal instincts tear their way to the surface in a flooded rush.

I track the scent, heart hammering, breathing forced and ragged, until my eyes land on her.

Perfection. Tall for an omega. A wispy thing with a cloud of beautiful dark red hair and wide, light green eyes.

My primal surges forward in a final, desperate attempt to claim, to mark, to protect. When our eyes meet, her attention lands on me, and something in me literally shifts, like a missing piece physically snapping into place. Our recognition bond, I realize; our initial mating bond snapped into place. The rest of the world fades away along with the primal fog that's gripped me, as a sense of home and rightness settles. My entire life, I knew something was missing. Maybe I was chasing something unattainable. Now I know I had only been waiting. Waiting for her. My Omega.

Mine.

The word pounds through my skull. The haze that's taken me further evaporates as she jumps behind Remi, gripping his shirt. I realize in the next second of clarity that she's terrified of the deep, guttural growl that's emitting enough strength to make the hair on my own arms stand up. Fuck.

It's not my growl that she's scared of.

"CALDER." I infuse the word with my bark. It won't affect him like it would an omega, but it should do enough to snap him out of the haze that's gripping him hard. If he scares her anymore, or does something he'll regret later, he'll never forgive himself.

11

Calder

Honey and wild-grown florals dusted with brown sugar envelope me, seizing every bit of my attention. Every part of me that makes me an alpha homes in, desperately searching for the source. A dense black fog seeps into the edges of my vision, the rest of my senses following in a heightened state. Breathing in deeply, my lungs expand to capacity, longing and desperate for more. The candied, floral signature is drenched in a creamy and sweet undercurrent that has my primal growing feral.

Then, I see her.

Mine.

I'm beyond rational thought. A sense of rightness and undoubtable knowing blanket every inch of my skin, sending goosebumps racing so fast it feels like lightning lifting the coarse hair on my arms as it washes over me. My inner alpha lunges forward with so much force that my muscles brace on instinct in a last ditch attempt at maintaining any sense of decorum. As the seconds tick by, any efforts on my end crumble. A growl escapes my throat from deep in my chest; a show of my strength and ability to protect her. A show of my power as the lead alpha of our pack. A threat to anyone who'd dare harm her.

Movement at the edge of reality briefly catches my attention, indecipherable murmurs not fully reaching my ears. Everything in me demands that I move, that I claim, bite, provide, protect.

Mate.

My body shakes with restraint, fingers and hands flexing at my sides, my breathing heavy as she moves. My gaze follows, tracking every inch of her, watching as she shakily shuffles behind another alpha. My growl intensifies, ready to fight for her.

Threat.

Wide eyes and parted, lush lips peek out from behind the male's arm. Fuck, that scent. Her signature scent is screaming at me to touch, taste, to pull her to my chest hard enough that no force or being on earth could tear us apart. The twisted, burnt scent of fear reaches me, and I feel my head lower in the effort to protect my neck against whatever threat comes, to protect my mate from whatever is causing the anxious edge of panic permeating from her.

I vaguely recognize as she moves and watches me that... I'm the source of her fear. That can't be right. She has to know that I would never hurt her?

The small part of me still in control pushes back to the forefront. I clench my teeth, forcing my primal back by sheer will and trained strength, but our fated connection still lingers in the space between us. And nothing, no one, is taking her from me.

"CALDER."

My packmate's voice pulls me nearly completely out of the haze that's gripped me, and guilt swamps me in monstrous proportions, washing over me terrifyingly quickly. The energy I was pulling drains with the blood from my face, leaving me dizzy. I scared my mate; the woman I know without a shadow of a doubt, that I would do anything for. I put that look on her face, the burnt edge of fear in her sweet scent.

"Omega..." I look away from her as she hides behind my dad, his shirt in a death grip between her small, feminine hands. Not a threat, not an unknown alpha; my dad. A barely leashed silent promise hits me hard as Remi meets my eye, his own narrowed with rage. Fuck. I messed this up completely.

I only hope I haven't ruined our chance for her to trust us, her mates.

Because if she's mine, she's most likely Sage's scent match, too.

12

Opaline

Fear grips me as violent shivers wrack my entire body, the thought *run, run, run* a loop that fails to manifest, but urges my knees. My hips and knees are locked; any part of my body normally blessing me the ability to move is now frozen with a new thought: Alphas love the chase, and I can't leave this spot. My hands shake as I hide and cower completely behind Remi, fistfuls of his shirt wrapped and twisted in my fingers. His scent is shoved into my nose, forehead resting against him. Somehow in this insane situation, the alpha I've known all of one night is now my source of comfort, chocolate-covered cherries trying and failing to calm me.

The growl from the big one stops abruptly after the black haired one barks what I can assume is his name. I chance another peek, just slightly past Remi's bicep, at the two alphas across from us. Something close to devastation shows on the big one's face, a quiet *"Omega..."* free falling from his lips. It strikes a part of me that the sound is awe laced in sorrow. But that completely contradicts the deeply primal, threatening sound he was just releasing, practically loud enough to rattle the bottles of alcohol behind the bar not five seconds ago.

"What the hell was that, Calder! Go cool the fuck off outside! Jesus christ. What's gotten into you?" Remi's muscles are tense under the shirt pulled taught in my hands.

Seconds pass as he stands utterly still, swallowing deeply as he looks on between us. "I—yes, sir." The door shuts softly as he steps outside, leaving us alone with just the black haired one.

"Now, damn it Sage, can you keep yourself under fucking control, or do you need to leave too? I called your pack here to help her, not traumatize the poor thing even more," Remi barks. The strength of it causes me to jump even though I know it's not directed towards me.

"Yes. One hundred percent. Don't be upset with Calder, please. It's just... I mean, she's..." His wide eyes zigzag between Remi and me, mouth at a loss.

"What?" he asks, shortly.

"Mate...she's our mate." He whispers the words in the silent bar, but they hit me hard enough that he could've shouted them next to my ear, sending chills skittering over my skin and pulling a gasp from my lungs. At once, it's like an elephant is sitting on my chest, my lungs struggling to capture air as my knees shake and threaten to give out completely, static floating at the edges of reality.

Mate.

Impossible...there's just no way. I've already accepted that I won't ever have mates or a pack or the life omegas dream of, that our biology screams for.

It can't be true. I just don't understand. Even if it were true, wouldn't I be able to scent them? That's what I was always taught at the Facility. The immediate knowing when you see your fated alphas, your soulmates, comes through their signature scents. The main source of recognition.

A voice interrupts my jumbled thoughts as they trip over the other for the limited space in my brain. "Well, shit. Who am I to separate an alpha from his omega? Come on, pup." Remi's voice is lightened, an astonished and happy air to it as he turns and wraps a large hand over my shoulder, pulling me out from behind him. Twisting around him, it's not the one in front of me that catches my eye first. No. It's the one sitting on his haunches out front through the bay of windows, pulling at his hair, looking like he's going to be sick, or just was. Something in me urges me to go to the stranger, to stop whatever it is that's hurting him, making the giant alpha destressed.

"Hey, sweetheart..." The one in front of me bends down onto a knee, a concerned but almost boyishly hopeful expression painted onto his stunning face.

Two things happen simultaneously as his scent finally hits me without Remi's cherries monopolizing my nose: the all-knowing, soul-level truth that this alpha in front of me is mine, and the feeling of strong, warm arms wrapping around me as an uncontrollable whine breaks free from my throat. Nestling my nose where his scent is the strongest, breathing is its own battle between taking deep huffs and the stronghold that tension has with its fist around my ribs. But the space between my nose and the junction of his neck housing the warmth from my many exhales only seems to enhance his signature. Citrus, amber, and whiskey crash into me just as I feel our recognition bond snap into place, my weight relying on this alpha to keep me steady. My breath becomes strangled as my mind fights to process the impossible being presented on a platter.

Recent fate hasn't thrown me anything but scraps; survival on my best days, suffering on my worst. I had stopped believing a pack would ever want me or choose me, let alone that I'd find my one perfect, fated mate after so long. No...not one. *Two.*

Mates.

The weight of gravity finds me again as he sets me on my feet. I hadn't even noticed he'd picked me up. His cheek nudges my own, marking me with his scent, marking me as his. Tears stream down my face, and he pulls back to wipe them away with his thumb. "I've got you." Three words that make my chin wobble, more tears threatening to spill over. Over his shoulder, though, I see his packmate pacing outside in front of the bay of windows at the front of the bar. I can't explain with words the pull he has on me. I know he's mine, too, even without having scented him. Every cell in my body urges me to go to him.

"Go on, sweetheart." He releases me enough for me to step back slightly, my eyes locked on the man outside. "I promise Calder would never hurt you. He's a giant teddy bear. Pretty sure he'd rather rip out his own heart than hurt you. He's in his head about his reaction to meeting you. To finding you, little omega. His primal hit him hard, but don't hold it against him. Please." It wasn't entirely a question, but I find myself nodding anyway, rewarded with a tiny hint of a smile tilting one side of his lips before I move to step past him. His hands fall gently as his eyes shine, like it's a struggle to let me go. Honestly, I feel the same, even with the pull from outside.

Letting go of the worn brass handle, I step through the entryway into the morning sunshine, on the walkway in front of Remi's bar. The small chime above the door signals to the giant alpha that someone's come to join him. Although he doesn't even look my way.

"Dad, just—" His voice sends shivers dancing across my skin, the depth and pure masculine tenor calling to my inner omega. Midway through his sentence, the wind shifts, ruffling my hair forward and drawing my scent towards him, his words coming to a halt. I have no doubt he now knows it's not his dad that's standing here, but me. Whirling up to his full height from his crouched position, he faces me. A look of...terror, and what feels an awful lot like longing, is reflected back at me.

His chest rises and falls in a noticeably odd rhythm, like he's trying to tamper his breathing, to keep himself rooted to the spot he stands, still as a statue. His eyes, breathing, tension lining every inch of his strong body gives the illusion of control. As though if he takes one step, he won't stop. Suddenly, with that image, it's all I want: to be wrapped in his strong arms. I should objectively be terrified, should be running as far as possible, as quickly as I can. But a curious warmth and nudge from my inner omega settles those thoughts, leaving me with instinctual confidence that he's safe. His bright, golden eyes burn fiercely into me, but, there's something else there, something much softer that I wonder how much of the world gets to see from this large, intimidating alpha. The lost romantic in me dares to wonder if this part of him could maybe just be for me. Just for his omega. *His.* The thought is overwhelming.

I wait for him to do something, say something, move to me, make literally any concrete inclination he wants me. But as time ticks by, he doesn't. The whine that slips free as my shoulders curl inward is sudden and solely my omega. Maybe I'm misreading him.

He doesn't want me?

13

Calder

I will not fuck this up a second time.

Effort to keep my body coiled tight, not moving, and as unthreatening as possible is overwhelming. If I could shrink myself in this moment, I would, if it made her feel safer. I focus on my breathing, giving the sweet woman before me the chance to control the situation and come to me of her own accord, should she wish to. I won't...I can't terrify her again.

Raw possession and determination lace my every breath at the thought, and I fight my alpha for dominance to stay fully present. But I know one thing: both my inner primal and I are both ready to tear through anything that could harm our mate.

I have a mate.

Seconds trickle by morphing into a lifetime as silence stretches between us, and I start to immediately second-guess everything as doubt slithers in. The idea that she doesn't want me, that I've already ruined this before it even began, or maybe she's just coming out here to tell me she just wants Sage, my packmate. The charming, playful one she can feel comfortable with. The rehearsed lines telling her if he's what she wants, I won't stand in their way are already preparing themselves in my mind. Because that's exactly what I'd do; I would let Sage find happiness in our mate alone and step away from the pack, while doing what needed to be done. I know it to be true, just as I know she's meant to be mine, whether she wants me or not. Racing thoughts of bonded illness start forming, broken off with a siren's call.

The distressed whine that envelopes every particle separating us pulls my attention back to the moment, hair raised, and knuckles white. Any controlled resistance snaps, breaking inside of me. Some cross between a growl and a purr shakes my chest as two long strides eat the distance between us. I have her in my arms, legs wrapped around my sides in what feels like under a second. The urge to fix what's causing her harm, even if it's me, is overwhelming and a call I will never deny. My job is to protect, and if I can't even do that, knowing I'm the source of her fear, what good am I for her?

An alpha's bark may momentarily control and command an omega. But an omega's distressed whine demands the attention of an alpha to fix and protect by any means necessary, especially for mates.

Her muscles seem to loosen slightly, relaxing her full weight in my arms as I hold her head with one hand, her bottom with the other. Her gods damned scent wraps around me, and this close, directly from the source, goes straight to my cock. The heat radiating between her thighs does nothing to calm the images of my knot sliding into her pussy from my mind.

Fuck. I shake my head as if I could physically dispel the despicable thoughts clouding my brain, the primal urges of pleasing my mate in all ways taking hold. The chanted demands to claim, bite, and rut are still in the back of my mind, urged on by my primal.

I know the moment she takes her first breath of my scent, though. The impact of our recognition bond snapping into place nearly bowls me over. The sensation is just a tiny fraction of what it will feel like once I sink my teeth into her and can eventually claim her, tying our souls together. I squeeze her to my chest and hope to god she'll accept me.

The soft, almost hesitant touch and nudge against my cheek as she scent marks me makes me clench my teeth, pulling her tighter. I hold her head in place, nuzzling against her gently and thoroughly making it more than clear she owns me, without the words. "Thank you, little omega." My lips land where her ear meets her cheek in a kiss I hope holds the magnitude of my gratitude, not wanting to break contact. "Thank you for the second chance."

I feel the breath she takes as warmth tickles my skin just before pulling back to look me in the eyes. Hers are a mesmerizing light green that perfectly oppose her beautiful deep red, almost brunette hair. She feels calmer, if not still a little understandably overwhelmed. The second she graces me with a shy smile, it's like the fucking sky explodes in glitter and streamers. I can't control the huge dopey smile she gets from me in return. I wonder if she has any clue just how wrapped around her finger I am already.

My literal dream come true.

14

Opaline

The feeling of being in Calder's arms is like finally finding home again. Another reminder that my spirit, my essence of being, has been lost and lonely for so long that I forgot what it meant to be wanted. After my mother died, I lost both of those essential feelings, growing more numb and defeated over time.

Until I presented as an omega. A new spark of hope had ignited within me all those years ago. A dream that, as an omega, I would almost certainly find my mates and know what it is to love and be loved. I'm not saying it's right or even remotely fair to everyone, to other designations, looking and waiting for love. But it's the realistic lens of life as an omega. We're taught we're rare and by default are in high demand by countless alphas looking to complete their packs. The amount of money and donations the O.C. Facilities collect from packs desperate to find their mates is a direct reflection of that.

Over the course of ten years at the Omega Facilities, week after week, month after month of not being chosen, of not finding that magic I was taught about, I gave up on that, too. And when that too ended, what was the point? All I had was the instinct to survive another day. But for what? There was nothing but fear, numbness, helplessness, and the unending plea to the universe to end it all. Now I know why. I've been waiting for this day. For this exact moment to finally find me.

I've melted against his wide chest, my body giving into a call so primal and magical, it's like it was written in the stars. And truly, I guess it was. My scent match, my fated mate. Feeling everything coursing through me so deeply, I don't realize that he's brought us back inside.

Sage joins us, cuddling at my back, a steady and bright mirror of Calder's protective hold. The soft touch of his lips as he kisses my ear and temple sends an entirely new kind of warmth through me. I can't help the sigh of relief and release of compounded weariness that leaves me as their scents wrap around me completely.

I hear more than see Remi coming back into the room, clearing his throat. He explains he'd briefly stepped into his office to make a couple of phone calls. I manage to open my eyelids that weigh ten pounds each and see a loving smile on his face as he takes in the sight of the three of us. I owe this to Remi. The entire night, the entire last twenty minutes that have changed the course of my life forever, in the best way. It's all because of him opening his heart to help me.

"Well. This changes things a little, I guess." He chuckles, sitting down on a stool, resting a forearm against the wooden bar top. "What's the plan now, then? I guess if Opaline doesn't need a job at your resort, I assume she'll move in with you?"

My attention snaps up, and I blink a few times to clear my eyes of the sleepy fog that had taken hold. "Job?"

"Don't worry, sweetheart. That was just our original plan when we came out here. Rem had called Calder, and after we got here, the plan had been to offer you a job at our resort and give you your own room in our seasonal staff lodging quarters. Just to kind of help get you on your feet again, see how we could help." Sage steps back, and I immediately miss the warmth he provided, the chill of the air too cold now without him. He goes to sit next to Remi, and he must read my thoughts because he shoots me a charming smile and a wink that makes me blush and bite my lip, forced to look away.

"What was the job? Can I still have it?" I ask.

Calder leans back to look me in my eyes, and his brow furrows, making his angular, severe face adorably confused. With a hand on my back soothingly, he tells me, "Babygirl, you don't have to have a job at all if that's what you're worried about. We'll take care of anything you could ever want. We're not saying you can't have a job, of course. But if there's a sense of obligation on your part, there shouldn't be. Okay?" I almost melt completely at the pet name slipping from his lips and force myself to listen and focus. How long had I dreamed of the sweet pet names my future mates and I would share?

"I appreciate that. But, honestly...I think I'd really like to have a way to contribute and something to focus my energy towards. It would make me feel good about myself, especially after the last few weeks. At least for now, for a while?"

"Of course, little one. The choice and the decision are always yours. Just know you have options." Sage nods and smiles.

"Opaline, you could tell these idiots to jump in heels, and they'll ask 'how high?' with hearts in their eyes. They're wrapped around your finger more than you could possibly know, pup." Remi laughs loudly, a hand to his chest, like it wasn't his own joke. I can't help but laugh a little too simply at his joy, trying to hide it at the expression on Calder's face.

"Tempting...just curious," I hum, a flush creeping up to my cheeks, "how high do you think they could go?" I joke back and fully let myself absorb the radiating happiness, for the first time in as long as I can remember. Happiness rises in me, leaving a soft, residual high.

Sage laughs in return, clapping his hands together and waggling his long finger. "Oh, this is dangerous. She's realizing her powers too soon." Calder taps my behind lightly, but I don't miss the light in his eyes.

"Alright, alright. Well, in that case, would you like to have your own room for a while at the resort still? That was the original plan, too. You're more than welcome to stay at our place with us, just up the mountain a little. It's your house too, now." He says the last sentence a little more gently, softer, its weight and significance clearly not missed by anyone in the room. It serves as harsh grounding reminder that I'm filthy and have been sleeping under a tarp.

God, it hits then how they must see me. I mean, really see me. This isn't the well-fed, clean, and pretty girl from the Omega Care Facility. They're getting the malnourished, dirty, pathetic version. The wave of nausea is overwhelming, accompanying shame all encompassing. The following embarrassment surely not to be short-lived. I'm positive part of them is disappointed that I'm their omega. Of all the beautiful women it could have been, they got saddled with me. This version of me. "Hey, hey. What just happened? Where'd you just go in that head of yours, omega? Your scent just turned...burnt."

Calder eyes me with concern. But, I just can't bring myself to point out to them that I see it too and understand how deeply disappointed in me they must be. I'll have to prove I'm worthy of them when we get to their resort. Get myself back to decent looking, and show them how dedicated I can be through the job they gift me with. I can be a good omega for them, I can. "Nothing to worry about. But, umm, in this case, I'd like to have my own room at the resort while I get settled back into a regular routine and feel more like myself." I notice myself trying to sit up a little straighter, a little more proper, tucking my dirty hair behind my ears and smoothing it a little as a polite smile forcefully paints itself upon my face.

"Uh, yeah, sweetheart. Anything you want," Sage responds a bit slowly, as Calder stays quiet. I can feel his eyes on me through his silence, though. I'm sure the weight of his gaze will always be known by me and my inner omega. Not simply because of his naturally emitted power, but because he's my lead. "This will uh, give us the chance to court you properly then, too. Ya know? Like we would have had we met through the Omega Facilities, like most packs." Sage smiles at me reassuringly. "It'll be great."

15

Sage

The sweet woman in my arms rests peacefully, breaths heavy and even. I'm the lucky bastard who gets to sit in the back seat with her while Calder drives us back west, back to our home. Or, I guess the resort lodging, since it sounds like that's what she wants for now.

It stings a little that she doesn't want to move in with us and start our life together. I'm ready to jump in head first, right now. Get her nest all set up, buy her everything she could ever want, and figure out what treats she likes. Hell, I'll get her a whole litter of puppies if it'd make her smile. Calder and Adrian would get over it. The thought makes me smile.

But I understand why she needs space to herself for a while. I really do. I quite literally cannot imagine what the last several weeks have been like for her. Hell, we don't even know her story before that or what it was like growing up, or what the Facility was like for her. I want to know everything. Every day of her life that I had to miss. Realistically odds are against meeting straight out of the womb, but tell that to my overbearing inner alpha.

The image of staying up late into the night, brushing her hair, sharing ice cream under the stars, snuggled under a blanket, lights up in my mind, and god damn, I can't wait for moments like those. Hopefully forever, for the rest of our lives. Fuck, the emotion that's been building all night and day finally must reach its peak because it's all bubbling over. Fighting the thickness in my throat and heat behind my eyes does nothing. Silent tears fall, coating my lashes. I just wipe them away and sniff quietly so I don't wake her. Resting my head against the seat rest behind me, I keep one hand in her hair, stroking her, the other gripping my roots at my scalp. Like the small tugs can keep me grounded.

"Hey, you okay man?" Calder meets my eyes in the rearview mirror, concern etched into his brow as his golden eyes reflect back at me.

I nod. "Yeah. I'm good. Great, actually. Perfect. I just... I guess it's all hitting me, ya know? I just can't believe after so many years we finally have the center of our pack; our scent-matched soul-mate." I take a deep, slow breath before continuing. "I just, I can't help but let my mind wander about what she's been through. What the last few weeks have been like for her and everything she's had to do to take care of herself completely alone. I know it's illogical, but, part of me is so angry with myself that I wasn't there to protect her."

He reaches a hand awkwardly back to grip my ankle, a gentle touch from my pack lead, to settle me. "You're already doing everything you can to be the best alpha for her. You're taking care of her and making sure she's warm and comfortable and safe. She's fed. I have complete faith in you, Sage. If I weren't here, I know you'd be exactly what she'd need, all on your own. You're *her* fated mate, too, brother. Don't forget that." Fuck, I just nod my head in silence, emotion clogging my throat. That's the thing with Calder. He somehow always knows what each of us needs, what we need to feel supported, need to hear. Even when he and I were teenagers, he always possessed the qualities of a lead.

"Thanks, man. I appreciate it."

My mind drifts and wanders a little more as we sit in comfortable quiet. A calming voice revealing the upcoming weather forecasts murmurs softly against the hum of the wind as we drive. "What about the others?"

"Exactly what I was just thinking about." He huffs. "I realized we hadn't even mentioned Adrian or Everette to her at the pub. I think my alpha had me tied up for a while, even after my mind mostly cleared." He runs a hand over the lower half of his face, releasing a soft breath that might be a hint of a laugh. "Everette is going to pass out from happiness. It's Adrian that I have to admit, I'm a little worried about... Not that I think he would ever hurt her. I hope that's obvious. I just worry what this might trigger for him and his...coping mechanisms. Not to mention..." He sighs.

"What?" I push, waiting for him to continue.

"It's not entirely unheard of for an omega to only scent match one or two alphas in a pack." I start to open my mouth to protest, but he gently cuts me off with a glance in the rearview. "I'm not saying that's going to happen here. And, even if it did, we'd still have the chance to be a great pack, all together. I just think we should be mindful of multiple potential outcomes given she hasn't scented Ever or Adrian, yet."

"Hmm..." I don't want to tell him that's bullshit. I know in my heart we're all her matches. I can't tell you how, but I just feel it. He probably does too. I'm sure this is just his way of keeping balance to the situation. "When's Ever get back? Should we just call him? I hate to give this kind of huge news over a phone call, but what other choice do we have?"

"We most likely can't even do that. He'll be gone for a bit longer. This one's a ten-day trip, I think. No, maybe a fourteen-day trip? Either way, he doesn't have access to his phone. We'd have to call the Retreat Center. But even then, they might not take messages depending on what he included in his preliminary paperwork. If he only allows us to be in contact in the situation of severe injury or death for a packmate or family... I think we're out of luck until he comes home."

"Fuck."

"Yeah, fuck. Hopefully, he soaks up as much zen energy as he can now. Because our entire lives are about to change forever, in beautiful ways." Everette does an annual silent retreat practically in the wilderness. They're never ten to fourteen days, though.

"God, I can't imagine being in complete silence for that long." At least they do group meditations and silent activities like painting and things. But that only eats up so much time. What the fuck else is he doing? *Thinking?* Christ. The thought alone makes me wanna shiver.

"Of course you can't, Sage. I have no trouble believing that." He chuckles, and I do all I can to not wake our girl, rolling my eyes in the rearview mirror. Which only makes him smile bigger.

"But, seriously, what the hell is he doing for that long, alone, in complete silence? You think he talks to himself when no one else is around?"

"He does it here. I don't know why he wouldn't somewhere else. I'm sure they're allowed to speak when they're alone. That'd be a mindfuck after a week or two if not." He grunts at the thought, and I absolutely agree.

"He does talk to himself kind of a lot, huh?" I smile. "I think our princess here will love all his quirks," I whisper, leaning down slightly. "And you don't even know yet that you have two other alphas, huh, sweet omega?"

16

Opaline

The image I had in mind from the way the guys described their resort to me comes entirely short of the breathtaking reality I'm trying to comprehend. Everything is so....unbelievably stunning. And very obviously well maintained and cared for. The staff and people we've passed have been incredibly friendly with Sage and Calder, too, which is a good sign. Not that I really needed confirmation. But it's still reassuring in my instincts and natural inclinations to want to trust them.

They said I'd get a full tour in a bit. But, just walking through the grounds as they each point in different directions, naming where certain things are located is already overwhelming. I don't think I have ever even seen natural hot springs in a movie or anything. So, this all is surprising and a little unexpected in itself. Just from our quick walk through the area leading to my room, they'd pointed out a spa, clubhouse for games with a food hall, a venue they rent out for events and weddings, a beautiful courtyard, and various indoor and outdoor natural hot springs. I just can't seem to wrap my head around the fact that they *own* this entire place and keep it running. It seems unreal.

The lingering scent of mineral-rich, sulfuric waters floats through the space around us, serving as a constant reminder of where we are and even the reason why: the natural hot springs. Soft trickles and echoes of flowing water and happy laughter of resort guests surround us as we walk. Birds chattering, and the insects doing whatever it is they do to produce noise work together forming a symphony of calming, constant hum of nature.

This place just may be heaven. My inner omega is absolutely preening at the idea that this may be our home and the place we'd be spending our time now, with our alphas. I, on the other hand, am trying to keep a more level head. I have to prove myself first. Maybe even more so now that I see how successful they really must be, owning such a naturally luxurious space. I don't have to see their home to know it'd compare to what's before me.

Calder's thumb gently strokes my hand as we walk, connected, side by side. A winding path led us to a polished, log...mansion? That's the best way I can describe what I'm looking at. It's a beautiful, huge, two-story building that looks like it was made out of logs, literally. But it's smooth and shining under the sun's rays. Dark green shutters sit beside each window, manicured trees and landscaping along the path, and there is even a cute patio area in the front with fluffy seating and a small metal fire pit. It's different than the obvious luxury that was the main resort lodging building we had walked past briefly. More down-to-earth. It gives me such a good feeling just walking up to it. Warmth and bubbly hope wash over me, bringing goosebumps with that cascade over my skin. As seconds pass, the sensation only grows until I'm fighting back tears of rising relief and happiness. The weight of everything I've been carrying so desperately wants to fall, but I can't bring myself to let it go quite yet.

Sage opens one of the two large doors that sit together, comprising the entrance. Immediately walking in, we're bathed in warmth. There's a large, assumedly communal living space with several couches, a huge TV, and shelves lined with games, puzzles, and books. The open room is entirely empty and devoid of others. Which I hate to admit, is a bit of a relief. Everything was starting to feel like too much, again.

Sage saunters past and stands in the middle of the room with a grin and his hands on his hips. "This is our on-site employee lodging. Not everyone lives here, obviously. Most live in town. But, we have some people that prefer to stay here, and we have some staff that come from out of state, or even out of the country sometimes, to work here for the summer or the busy season in winter through programs that we're partnered with."

I take in the room, all the details I missed on the first pass, and land back on Sage. "It's perfect." The minute look of concern that I hadn't noticed hidden under his bright smile evaporates at my words.

"You can stay here, or we can set you up in a room at the main lodge. Or..." His voice drops to more of a whisper. "...you can always come home with us. We can get your nest set up and pretty. I know we'd love to take you shopping...buy y—"

"Sage." Calder puts just enough power in his words to cut off his packmate. Not a bark, but close enough. Looking back down to me at his side, his eyes met mine, our joined hands now resting against his stomach. "The decision is yours, omega. We just want you to know you have options and want you to be settled where you'll be most comfortable. Forgive us if we seem too eager at times. We're still processing that this is real. That you're real."

God, he has no idea how badly I needed to hear those words. Just another confirmation I hadn't really known I'd needed. The whimper that escapes me is quiet. But Calder still catches it, gripping me to his chest in a hug. My arms wrap around him instinctually, and it feels so natural, like I'd fallen into his arms countless times already. The sensation of a deep familiarity is hard to explain and possibly even beyond explanation. But the comfort he so naturally offers is nearly addictive, so soon.

I scent Sage before feeling him, his lips landing on my temple. "Sorry, Opaline. I don't mean to overwhelm you. Forgive me?" I'm already getting so used to their pet names they'd used so easily with me that my own name doesn't sound quite right on his lips.

Pulling back, I hug him too, noticing the cloud of uncertainty now dimming the previously perpetual glow in his eyes. "There's nothing to forgive." I smile reassuringly. "But, if it's okay... I think I'd like to stay here. At least for now?" It's phrased as a question, but I already know the answer.

"Of course. Let's show you to your room." Calder leads the way to the left, down the hall.

17

Opaline

The room is perfect. There isn't a single thing I don't love about it, instantly.

It's small and cozy, putting me at ease. Omegas notoriously craved small, darkened spaces. Especially during heats. Hence, why nests were so important. A warm daydream of sinking my bare feet into the lush cream rug covering the beautiful hardwood floors greets me. The very thought of starting my mornings in such a soft, quiet, and safe space is a little too hard to grasp in the moment. The bed is perfect, too; not overwhelmingly large, but not a tiny, uncomfortable cot like I was accustomed to at the Facility for so long. And it's certainly not a blanket on the ground. I run my hand over the light green, textured fabric, Calder noting the movement. Only, the sneaking image of being cuddled up next to one of them in the small bed probably isn't what he's thinking about. The picture of the two huge alphas in the bed this size almost makes me laugh. If it became a battle, I think simply based on size, I'd have to bet on Calder, my lead alpha. I...have a lead alpha... the thought rocks me as it really lands, again.

"Don't worry. We'll get you softer bedding. Those probably aren't the best quality."

"No, it's great. Seriously, I don't need anything." I smile, hoping he can see the truth in my words. "Thanks for offering, though." I really did appreciate that they both noticed so much and seemed so eager to please since we'd met. A couple of black and white, large photos framed above the bed, of the mountains covered in snow, draw my attention. "Did one of you take those?" I nudge my chin towards the photos, admiring them. There's a trait I can't put my finger on, that makes me wonder if they aren't professional or printed in mass, sold in stores. They feel more personal and artistic.

"Ah, yeah. About that...that's actually a good segue into something else we wanted to talk to you about." Tracing my eyes over to Calder, he has a hand rubbing the back of his neck, looking almost nervous. A peek at Sage gives me nothing, because he's just grinning ear to ear. I can practically feel my spine stiffen with unease, though, trying to mask any emotion on my face. Just then, of all the moments his phone's been silent, Calder's rings. He mutters a curse and says, "It's our emergency maintenance," before even pulling it from his back pocket to check the name or number on the screen. I guess it must be a special ringtone. "Fuck, babygirl, I have to take this. I'm so sorry. Sage, fill her in on Everette...and Adrian." He answers with a harsh greeting, kissing my forehead as he passes me to stand in the hall, his voice getting quieter and quieter, as do his footsteps.

"Everette and Adrian?" I ask curiously, assuming they must be other employees or maybe the maintenance team he's on the phone with now.

"Yeah, princess. Come sit." He plops down on the bed and pats the spot next to him, waggling his eyebrows. His silly demeanor oddly makes me feel a little better. I make my way to him, and he pulls me in a little tighter than what might be comfortable for any two other people who've just met. But, we're not just two people, are we? We're scent-matched. Mates. Everything in me wants to trust and fall into him.

"Hi." The word is a soft whisper as it spills unconsciously from my lips.

"Hi, sweetheart." His eyes soften, and a gentleness tips his lips as he studies my face. "Screw Calder. Come here." He pulls me onto his lap, and honestly, it's like any weight that I'd been carrying is suddenly taken off my shoulders and chest. I can't help but to melt into his strong arms, resting my nose near his neck, scenting him from the source. His citrus, amber, and whiskey scent fills my lungs as a heavy contentment crashes over me, forcing a happy sigh. "Fuck, this feels good having you in my arms. You have no idea, Opaline. If I could stay here with you for the next week in this room with no interruptions, I would. Lock you away and keep you to myself." He sighs, the emotion behind the sound mirroring my own. "Calder would get grumpy, though." He whispers the last part, and I feel my lips press against his warm skin as my smile takes over. I like that it seems they have an easy relationship between them. Not all packs have the best dynamics.

Clearing the freshly-formed thickness in my throat, I push back a little to see his face. Bright blue, almost grey eyes meet mine in an instant. His black, curly hair falls messily across his forehead, and god, the sight of him nearly takes my breath away. This man is unbelievably beautiful. Where Calder is all raw power, carved like a severe god with golden eyes, and sun-kissed skin, this man is almost entirely opposing. He's a captivating contrast with light eyes, dark curls, and frankly, model-esque good looks. If I saw him in a magazine, I wouldn't be surprised. He exudes charm and confidence.

I want all his smiles and playful winks directed at me. He's a few inches shorter than Calder, but still towers over me, even at my height. Six-five, maybe? Tracing his face, I'm captivated by the perfect butterfly in the center of his upper lip.

One of those devastating smirks makes an appearance, and I realize I'm already deep under his spell, caught on the perfection that is his mouth.

"If you keep staring at my lips like that, I'm going to do something I was told not to." My eyes jump back up to his, and I can see the playfulness lingering there, hear it in his teasing voice. It's exactly what I need, and I feel it bringing a buried part of myself I'd lost long ago, back to life. Feelings along a spectrum I hadn't thought myself capable of experiencing anymore.

"And what might that be?" I ask innocently, tilting my head to the side for good measure, exposing my throat a little in the act. God help me, I want to tease this alpha. His growl vibrates through his chest pressed against mine, the sound calling to my omega. A whimper escapes me, and I work to press my thighs together to stop my scent from overtaking the room as I start to perfume. His fingers start their slow journey sliding up my thigh, only feeding the fire that refuses to be put out, as he leans in closer.

"My omega's naughty, isn't she?" Sage's voice is a low, heated rumble. "A little, sweet, innocent tease trying to get her alpha in trouble with our pack lead, huh?" The combination of his words, scent, and tenure breaks past the thin barrier I was hiding any hesitations behind. He somehow knows the second my resistance snaps.

We both move, leaning into our instincts, as all reservations are lost and our mouths suddenly meet. The fullness and lush softness of his lips overtake mine with an amount of passion only an alpha could truly give. My alpha.

The warmth of one big hand squeezes my hip, the other cupping my jaw with unexpected tenderness, even as he kisses me with a primal, hungry desperation that matches my own. He swallows my muffled whine, taking me in a claiming that lights me up, throwing gasoline on the fire, sending a blazing heat to the best places. All the words we haven't yet said are being devoured and expressed physically.

God, this man knows how to kiss. Just as I feel myself ready to push back, push for more, I feel everything shift. Just as quickly as it began, his lips slow and soften. His grip lessening.

The fire fades slowly to embers, and I feel the way he exhales after our kiss like he's been holding his breath and can finally breathe. Boy, do I understand the feeling. His hand strokes down from my jaw to the side of my neck, brushing gently over my pulse.

Pulling back, he rests his forehead to mine, taking another slow, deep breath. "Shit, I didn't want to rush that. Are you okay, sweetheart? Too much?"

I blink, a little dazed still from the intense moment we just shared. "Not at all. You didn't. Rush things, I mean." Looking down at me, his smile's gentle, crooked, and glowing so brightly it lights up his face enough to make my omega purr with satisfaction.

"I've wanted to do that since the second I walked into Rem's pub and saw you."

A throat clears, and I hear clothing shuffle behind me. I suck in a breath, jumping in Sage's lap to see Calder's massive form now filling the doorframe, watching us as what feels like a flood of emotions passes through his face before landing on a smile. "Looks like maybe I should've ignored that call, huh?"

18

Adrian

A FEW MOMENTS AGO

"This better be an actual emergency." Calder practically grunts into the phone, skipping a *normal-people* greeting.

"Hello to you, too, asshole." I bunch my brows together in agitation and curiosity as to what's up his ass. Something churns in my stomach, making me feel like I'm on the downside of a high rollercoaster. I wonder if it has to do with why they were both gone last night. I'd been on a late-night ride on my bike and couldn't sleep, on the road until the early morning hours. Like ants were battling it out under my skin, I just couldn't fucking relax. I've felt off since, too. Seeing their private quarters' doors wide open and one of our SUVs gone was completely unexpected. Something's up.

He sighs deeply and starts tripping over his words, which is not like him. "I just, well, anyway, first— what's going on? There's a reason you called." I'm the one who grunts back this time, a little unimpressed with his answer.

"Pipe broke behind the East Springs Lodge. If we don't fix it now, it could fuck up the greenhouse system and leave the events venue and spa without running water this weekend. You seeing any pressure issues on the Northern buildings?"

"Shit. Okay. Yeah, Jewel texted and mentioned the spa showers were less than stellar this morning. I just assumed it was a filter issue and thought it could wait. Nothing about the Main Lodge, thankfully, though. So North should still be fine."

"Definitely more than that," I huff, wondering where the hell his head is at. "I just walked the back slope. Depending on how bad it is, we might have to shut down the North line too, which would be a shitshow. And, I know Annabelle's got the venue rented out for a wedding."

"Fucking hell. Alright, we'll be right there. Can you grab supplies?"

"Yeah. I'm parked at the shed right now, already on it." There was silence on the other end for so long, I pulled back to check our connection. Something just wasn't sitting right with me. A too-long pause that hovered somewhere between professional and personal nearly welded my jaw shut. I knew, I just *knew* there was something my pack lead wasn't telling me. The damn pipe could wait another couple of fucking minutes. "Calder..."

He clears his throat and sighs again. "Listen, Adrian. I think we all need to sit down and talk, tonight."

Suddenly, it was like I couldn't stop the word vomit trying to slip from my lips in an effort to soothe my raging anxiety. "Where the hell were you guys early this morning? I came back, and the house was empty."

"We just have a lot to fill you in on." There it is. A lead weight hit my fucking chest. I can barely suck in a breath enough to respond with the dizziness and sick feeling hitting me.

"Say it. Now."

"I really think this would be better if we were in person for this conversation."

"Don't give me that shit. Just fucking say it, Cald." Because a part of me already knows what's coming. I've been waiting for it, selfishly hoping the day never actually came, like the asshole I am. Everything's felt wrong, and my gut knows why.

"Rem called me last night. He found an omega living under a wet tarp behind his bar." Even though the words make me angry enough to growl, I suffocate the sound before it can even begin. Despite my history and hatred for omegas, my very nature is drawn to them in a way my biology can't fully deny. Just another reason why I avoid them at all costs. I just can't stomach the thought of living through the past again. The images of Natalie's face bombard me, and I squeeze my fists and slam my eyes open and shut to recalibrate to my real-time surroundings.

"Let me guess. Unbonded?" I ask flatly, forcing my throat to work. Although it's not really a question. We both already know the answer.

"Adrian..." he whispers too gently. It pisses me off. I don't want his fucking pity. "She's ours. Our Mate." I stay silent, the weight of what he's saying landing and bringing a new level of numb with it. "The recognition bond snapped into place for both of us. She's our scent match."

"Yours and Sage's," I deadpan, roughly.

"And, most likely yours and Everette's too, brother."

"No." The denial comes out a little too sharply to be comfortable for either of us.

Calder's response hits just shy of a bark, and I swear I can somehow feel his shoulders straighten, the pack lead taking the front seat now. "You know the statistics as well as anyone, Adrian. It's not unheard of for an omega to only match a partial pack, but it's not exactly likely. You know, already, the truth of the situation; otherwise, you wouldn't be reacting like this. Lean into your instincts and your intuition. Please. For us, if not for her or yourself. Opaline's staying here on the property. So she won't be at the house. Yet. Just—"

"She doesn't know about me?" I cut him off.

"No... Not yet. She doesn't know about Everette either, though." I feel my lips curl in with unexpected jealousy and more than a little disgust at myself. The implications of my bond with Everette feel like a kick in the stomach with their force. She will have three dream alphas at her disposal. Everything about Calder, Sage, and Everette is the exemplification of an omega's walking vision board.

"Keep her away from the greenhouse." The pathetic, petulant response only earns me another sigh from my lead.

"Adrian, please listen to me. We love you, and no matter what, we will figure this out as a pack. I just ask that you lean into your primal and try to forgive yourself for the past." I nearly snarl, but he cuts me off before it can take root. "I hate having to be the one to say this. And, I know you already know better than literally anyone else. But, if you are scent matches, you know what will happen to her if you don't answer the mating bond."

"Easy then. I won't fucking scent her."

I hang up, nearly crushing the phone in my palm.

Not happening.

Omegas were for other men, other alphas. For people who didn't have hands that served as a constant reminder of how it felt to fail someone so small, sick, and fragile. To fail in protecting; the most important job I have as an alpha. I shove the truck door open harder than I intend, and it bounces back into my forearm as I climb out. My boots crunching over gravel as I move towards the maintenance shed is all I can focus on as flashes and flickers of haunted memories pull me down, drowning me. My pulse thuds in my ears as my surroundings fade in and out, muffling reality.

The entire night, and even this morning, I was alone, out on my fucking bike swerving like an asshole through the mountains. Anything to push back against the black cloud of thoughts that follow me, endlessly. And my packmates? They were rescuing their damn scent match like white knights. Their soul mate. *Theirs.* Not mine.

It hits then, really hits me what this will mean for our pack as a whole, and the bond we've built over so many years. I will avoid scenting her, being anywhere near the omega. There would never be a bond between us.

That only means that I'll have to leave my pack brothers, too. There is no way for her to live in our house, because she *would* be living there soon, without being in close quarters with her. There is no way to make this work. I can't even move to the staff lodging and continue working at the hot springs. I have no doubt this entire resort will quickly become her domain, too. The sick thought and comparison to other women trying to worm their way into our pack hits but instantly dies. Somehow, I know she's not one of the women trying to use our pack for money. The fact that I even thought it makes me sick and even more pissed at myself.

No, the only option is to leave at some point. It's just a matter of time and planning.

19

Opaline

Calder stands, filling the doorframe as I eye him. "Looks like maybe I should've ignored that call, huh?" he asks. I worry my lip a little, wondering if he's upset with me for kissing Sage and not him first as the pack leader. Anger wasn't one of the emotions I saw flitter across his face, though. Surprise, concern, even lust, maybe. Not anger.

Before my thought spiral can take root and bloom, he shoots me a wink and comes to sit on the bed next to Sage. Pulling one of my feet onto his lap, he palms my ankle possessively, long fingers holding and grounding me. The immediate calm that radiates through me speaks volumes on many things, and I find myself wanting to toss myself into his lap completely.

"I take it the conversation didn't get far?" Glancing at his packmate, humor lines his voice, but heat lingers in his eyes.

"Don't always need words, brother. Huh, princess?" A muffled, indecipherable response falls flat as I bury my head into his shirt momentarily. This shouldn't be a big deal. This is what happens in packs. And yet, I'm not sure why I suddenly feel a little shy with both their heated gazes on my skin. Each of them alone are overwhelming in their presence and attractiveness. But together? It's a lot, right now. The heat gaining real estate on my cheeks and chest is a direct reflection of that. "But, uh, no, we didn't quite get to the others," Sage continues, taking pity on me, with an evident chuckle. The two share a look, and I wiggle a little to sit up a bit more on Sage's lap, facing the two of them, causing Sage to grunt softly at the movement.

Calder reclines a little further and does nothing more than lightly pat his thigh before I'm moving without thinking, twisting to now chase comfort in his strong, steady arms and magic touch.

"Well, babygirl, we do have something important we need to talk about. We meant to mention it earlier when we picked you up from my dad's place. But, between the eventfulness of meeting, our alphas taking over, and then you falling asleep on the ride, it just hadn't come up. I'm sorry for that and for not telling you much sooner."

"Okay?" I say gently, a hanging question mark on the end as a tension in the air seems to build between all three of us. I can't say I care for it. "You're not kicking me out, are you?" I try to joke, but my stomach still flips, my body tensing and preparing for the worst.

"Never," Calder says quickly. "You will never be in the situation you just came from. I promise you that with all I am as your alpha."

Sage nods, increasing the grip he has on my hand momentarily. "It's nothing bad, sweetheart. It's just..."

"...It's just? What?" Anxiety squeezes my chest.

Calder's jaw ticks slightly, and he adjusts his position on the bed, moving me in his motions. "Omega, you're most likely not matched to one or two alphas."

My heart plummets, my chest tightening further, to a concerning degree. "What?" I felt our bonds snap into place, though...that can't possibly be true.

"There are four of us," Sage says softly, grinning.

"What?" I ask again, like a damn broken record, unable to get anything else out past my lips with the chaos storming under my skin.

"We have two other packmates, little one. Adrian and Everette." I blink, trying to process what Calder just actually said, and suddenly it's like I'm dizzy in the mist of a cloud.

"You're saying, I have two other alphas? Four alphas?" God, I sound idiotic to my own ears, like I can barely string together words or count on my fingers.

"We don't know that for sure just yet. But, the likelihood that they're your scent matches, too, is high. However, Opal, even if one or both of them happen to not be your matches, they will still be a part of your life. A part of our life, as a pack." I have absolutely lost my center of gravity. Four alphas...

"That's....a lot," I say lamely, more than a little dazed.

"I know. And, I'm sorry we have to hit you with it all at once. You've been through so much. But you deserve to know. And, it's really good news, babygirl."

I can't...god, I can't make sense of everything with the emotions and feelings flooding me. Just this morning, mere hours ago, I was literally living on the street, having given up hope on ever having a better life, certainly never finding the pack I had always dreamed of. Now...now, I have not one, not two, but potentially four scent-matched alphas.

A little too quickly, I pinch myself hard on the arm, making myself flinch before Calder grabs my hand away with a light growl. "None of that. No one's hurting you ever again, even yourself."

"I— sorry. I just wanted to make sure I wasn't dreaming. It all felt a little surreal. I just, I don't..."

"I know. We've got you." He pulls me in, even tighter, his scent washing over me easing the tension that'd taken over my shoulders and jaw. "We've got you."

"You have no idea how good it's about to get, sweetheart," Sage adds.

And that's just it, isn't it? The intense realization of how quickly everything can change hits me. Everything you are, everything you know, can shift in the span of a breath, a heartbeat, a blink. That's all the time it takes for your life to split in two. The before. And, the after. Everyone has their own; the moment that changes their life, leaving them in pieces. But, what if this is my chance at a new after?

My pulse flutters, caught somewhere between anxiety, excitement, exhaustion, and curiosity. "Are they like you two?"

Sage outright laughs, and it catches me off guard. "Not even close."

"Everette's a huge sweetheart. He keeps us all grounded and has the calmest energy of anyone I've ever met, much less an alpha. He'll love you instantly, and I have a feeling it'll be mutual." I really can't help but smile at that, mirroring Calder's. The excitement starts pushing its way to the forefront.

"And Adrian?" I ask, happily.

Their silence is loud.

"Uh." Sage rubs the back of his neck, glancing between Calder and me. "He's just a little complicated, is all."

"Adrian is one of the most devoted, trustworthy, protective people I've come to know. It's an honor to have him in our pack. I don't want you to have a skewed image of who he is at heart." Calder takes a deep breath, keeping eye contact with me. "However, he has experienced things in life that most simply have not. Much like you, omega. And it still affects him today. But that's not my story to tell you. It's his." He rubs my inner wrist softly. "Just, don't give up on him too soon, okay?"

I nod in blind agreement, but my brows are a little furrowed. I'm not sure what the hell to expect from this mystery alpha, to be honest. That didn't really paint a clear picture. I have questions bouncing around in my mind but can't seem to land on any just one. Before I can speak, Calder gets up, placing me gently back onto the bedding, still warm from where he sat.

"I'm so sorry, babygirl. But we have a maintenance emergency we have to deal with. I don't want you to feel like we just dropped this big news on you, uprooted your life, and then abandoned you to go work."

I raise my hand, standing up, and cut him off from continuing. "No, not at all. I completely understand." I shake my head a little, even though I really do agree and understand. "And, honestly. It's been an eventful night and morning. I'd really like to be able to shower and just...settle for a bit, while I adjust and sit with it all."

"Such a brave omega," Calder purrs, kissing the top of my head. I just melt at his touch, far too tempted to let him kiss me other places too. "You got it, sweetheart. Sage, you want to grab some fresh clothes for her from the laundry room? See if there's anything of ours over there the house attendant hasn't picked up and brought back yet?"

"Yep." Sage leans in and does what Calder didn't. He plants his lips so firmly against mine, I nearly fall over and start laughing from the impact before he grins and runs off down the hall.

Calder glances from my lips to my eyes with longing and a smile at his packmate's actions. As he starts to step back and speak, I grab his hand and stop him. "Wait..." He tilts his head with nothing but patience and waits for me to keep going. "Is... I mean. There's a chance I won't be..." I sigh deeply. "I mean, that I'm not Adrian's scent match?" I whisper the words. The ones that have been bouncing around in my head, fighting for dominance, fighting for me to just say them out loud. The little they've shared has only confused me and led me to wonder if this packmate of theirs is laughably different than them, what are the real odds he's my fated, perfect match?

Like he sees into my mind, directly to my thoughts, he says, "Or... you might be the *only* one who is his perfect match, little omega," just as softly in return.

20

Opaline

Yesterday, after the guys left, I explored the tiny bathroom that's adjoined to the room they put me in. I learned through Sage's excited chattering that not all of the staff rooms have private bathrooms and instead share a communal shower. I'm not sure I can put into words how relieved I am to not have to be one of those people. I get a pinch in my chest at the thought that just two nights ago, I would have been thrilled to even have that as an option. I would've been. I have to remind myself that being happy to have my own space doesn't mean I'm ungrateful, and try to have grace for myself in an overwhelming situation.

There were already tiny bottles of soap and shampoo waiting for me. I think I scrubbed every inch of myself three times over before just standing in the steaming hot water, thankful for the sensation of cleanliness. Even with the quick scrub down I tried to do in Remi's bathroom at his bar, I was still a level of dirty no omega would strive to be. The luxury of everything that was just being handed to me freely sat heavily.

I changed into the oversized clothes that Sage left for me and had been disappointed that they were clean and completely unscented. Luckily, I could still smell them on my bedding.

Running my hands over the smoothness of the sheets and the fluffiness of the pillows gave me a burst a giddiness. I had practically squealed from pure joy, bouncing my feet against the mattress like a little girl. God, it's been years, so long, since I've had a bed like the one in the room they gave me. Since the beginning of my time at the O.C.F.

Needless to say, I had created a makeshift nest to soothe myself as well as I could and passed out for the remainder of the day with Sparkles tucked tight against my chest. I woke up to dinner and a note on the small table letting me know it was from Calder and Sage, and they had wanted to let me rest and recoup without interrupting. They also provided an update on their maintenance issue that still needed attention. Based on the smell from the paper the note was sketched on, it almost seemed like they rubbed it against themselves. The thought still makes me smile this morning.

I had eaten in bed and then passed right back out. Only throughout the remainder of the night, I had both Sparkles and the note resting close to my nose. I should probably be more upset that they came into my room while I was at my most vulnerable, asleep. But, honestly? I'm not at all. The push our biology is driving us for overrides most of the common sense I should probably have about the situation. All I really can focus on is the fact that they went out of their way to provide for and check in on me. My alphas provided for me.

A knock on the door makes me jump, dropping the mass of hair I have in my hands about to put up in a bun, bringing me back to the present. "Jesus." I turn the corner in the small space and open the door to a very beautiful and well-dressed, petite blonde holding a clipboard. "Um, hi." I reach out my hand, and she follows the movement with a look that doesn't exactly feel friendly. "Annabelle, I take it?"

"Yes, that's me, in the flesh." She shakes my hand, but, in a way that makes it clear she doesn't want to be touching me. That's fine. Honestly, I'm starting to feel the same just within the few seconds I've known her. "The guys told me you were new and you'd like a little tour around the place. And, since I know it like the back of my hand, they couldn't think of anyone better."

The guys had also mentioned in their note that their special events manager would be dropping by at some point this morning for this exact reason. I'm really looking forward to seeing the rest of the beautiful resort. It'll be nice to get my bearings a little more before I start my new job. Which, I still don't know exactly what I'll be doing since it didn't come up in our limited conversation. But honestly, it doesn't matter. I will do damn near anything to make sure they see me as a better version of myself, worthy of them.

"Well, let's go then. I have a lot to do today." She eyes me up and down a little, with what feels like a forced smile towards me, surely noticing the guys' clothes I'm still wearing. In comparison to her fitted, flowered dress and shining, conditioned blonde locks, I can imagine why she'd be making that face towards me, now nearly a grimace. Everything else I have is simply too dirty. I'd embarrass myself more by wearing any item I'd brought with me here. So, blob of man-clothes it is.

"Of course, after you!" I say excitedly, more than ready to explore a little, despite her off-putting introduction.

From the moment I step outside, it's like an invisible bubble of energizing hope is floating me along the tour. The very real feeling of possibility follows me as we walk.

The signature scent and sounds of the sulfuric waters mingle with the nearby Fir trees and faint florals from the various flowerbeds on the grounds. Warmth soaks my skin despite the small chill that occasionally hits as the wind picks up here and there.

Although she may not be rushing to the top of my *most-liked* people list, Annabelle's voice is pleasant and smooth, if not a little curt, as she explains little bits about each building, spot, scenery, etc. to me. And, there is so much to see. Her spiel falls a little flat from her lips, every so often, but something tells me despite the fact her tour feels a little rehearsed, those unimpressed slips are a special treat simply for my being here.

The most impressive space that I've seen so far is the Main Lodge. It's a level of luxury that I would assume most people wouldn't expect from a hot springs resort nestled deep in the mountains. The interior is a beautiful combination of honey-toned timber beams and smooth, opulent cream. It's simultaneously rustic, charming elegance catches the sunlight from a multitude of windows, reflecting it on every surface. The exterior shows the building to be multiple stories and built with natural cut stones, perfectly placed. But, a big selling point is the giant stretch of floor-to-ceiling windows that span the entire height of the building, from the first floor to the highest on both the front and back of the building. They don't overly consume the entirety of its width, sitting just in the middle section of the tall exterior walls. The reflection of the glass perfectly mirrors the image of the natural surroundings. Trees and forest stretch far, climbing and covering the hills that comprised the towering mountains. It is, without a doubt, the most beautiful place I have ever been in real life.

At least it was, until now.

I follow behind Annabelle, the flow of her dress from the breeze halting as we step inside the newest building. The gasp that leaves my lips catches the attention of a couple of people in the steaming water nearest to us. Annabelle doesn't do a good job of hiding her eye roll, and in turn, I offer a silent apology to the couple. It's a quiet and calming space, clearly meant for relaxation.

I'd somehow found myself in what feels like a tropical island indoors. The water's scent is even more intense here, filling and compounding in every inch of the huge area. Dark stone covers the spaces between open pools of steaming spring water. There's one larger than the others nearest to the entrance, which I assume meant to act as a communal pool. But past that are smaller pools of water nearly hidden behind healthy, full palm trees and tropical plants and flowers, surrounding each one in semi-circles. Each new pod comes further into view as we walk the winding stone pathway. Every single inch of this place is literally covered in plants and greenery. Stopping for a moment, I glance up and realized we are, in fact, inside. The roof is a muted, frosted material that let in just enough light to know it was the sunlight shining through.

We reach the back and walk through an archway that leads both left and right; bathrooms and showers to one side and changing rooms and lockers to the other. There's a dark wooden station directly in the center, where we stand, that houses a glass cooler as well as stacks and stacks of towels. Annabelle reaches in and grabs a bottle of water, the plastic immediately coating in condensation from the invasive heat of the hot springs trapped inside. I realize how badly I want to grab one too, but she makes no effort to offer, and I don't know exactly how the system works here yet, or if there's a way I don't know of to track who takes what. I assume they're freely provided, but don't truly know. So, I leave it alone, instead whispering how amazing the indoor hot springs are, cautious to not interrupt the ambiance again.

The blonde sets down her clipboard and flips her hair over her shoulder as she takes a sip of water. For being shorter than me, she has a way of making me feel tiny. "I know. It really couldn't have turned out any better." She smirks, taking another sip, and honestly, I'm not exactly sure how to respond to that with the body language she's throwing towards me. So, I just wait to see if she continues. "My best friend, Vivian, and I helped design this place. Most of it was all our ideas. The guys basically did whatever we suggested. Like always, though," she chuckles and adds, "we've known them all for years at this point. This building in particular is Everette's *favorite."* She's practically humming with pleasure, eyes failing to entirely conceal an array of sparking arrogance.

The guys. That's not the first time she's said that. The implication is clear; she means Calder, Sage, Everette, and Adrian. My alphas. The sudden burst of jealousy hits me so hard I have to push my inner omega down to stop myself from scratching this woman's eyes out and pushing her into one of the pools.

The body language, the tone, the smirks, the unspoken insinuations all morning. I realize now exactly what she's been doing.

Hinting at the fact that she, or maybe her best friend, had a deeper relationship with my men other than working together.

I realize also, the exact moment she senses the change in me and my thoughts as her words finally hit their mark. The look on her face as she swings her sheet of golden hair again is nothing short of smug. She thinks she's won something by getting under my skin. Little does she know I spent too much time in a facility of nearly entirely female omegas. And some of them were as caddy as they come, from ultra-wealthy families. She's nothing I can't handle.

But, to be fair, those other women weren't hinting at relationships with my scent-matches... Taking a series of slow breaths, I follow the jerk in front of me out of the sanctuary that I hope to god I get to spend some more time in at some point. Without her ruining it.

And, I really, really hope Annabelle wasn't being truthful with her hints at a past I wasn't sure I could bear to know more of.

21

Sage

The non-stop bickering and grunts thrown between Calder and Adrian is starting to get on my last nerve.

Luckily, we were able to patch the job well enough for the event we had last night that rented out the venue. Really, it was just the bathrooms and small kitchen on-site that we needed to worry about. That just means we had to be up at four this morning to undo a few of the jimmy-fixes we had put in place temporarily to make it the few hours until the event was over, to re-do with permanent solutions before the next event that starts later.

To say I'm over this would be the biggest understatement of my life. I can't get my little omega off my mind. She's all I've been thinking about. If I had it my way, we'd be attached at the hip for at least our first week together. I was hoping to spend time with her last night when we dropped off dinner. She looked so exhausted and peaceful, all bundled up, sleeping, we couldn't bring ourselves to wake her up. No matter how hard my alpha was pushing for it. He wanted us to climb into bed with her and shimmy into that perfect place between her thighs so we could sleep on her stomach, wrapped up together. To both our disappointment, that didn't happen.

She's supposed to be getting a proper tour of the place, right about now. We couldn't show her the full spectrum of the resort yesterday ourselves unfortunately. Eyes bouncing around, I'm waiting for her to pop up somewhere so I can grab her and keep her to myself. Run us off into the woods at this point, hell.

I sigh heavily, toeing at the grass with annoyance written in bold across my forehead. Catching Calder's piercing side-eye, I realize my sigh must not have been quiet enough and caught his attention. Oops.

Looking between Adrian and me, he shakes his head minutely. "This isn't exactly where I want to be spending my time right now, either, alright? If you're going to be here, at least get off your asses and help," Calder starts, rolling into a mess of grunts and complaints I intentionally zone out.

"Crabby, Daddy Calder?" I try to tease, really I do. It's a years-long nickname that I know he hates. It comes out a little more deadpanned than I anticipate, just adding pressure to a mysteriously dormant volcano residing between the three of us. An indignant huff steals my attention, bringing me back to reality, dissolving the image of exploding lava my brain conjured.

"That's rich. I am fucking helping. I've *been* helping; arguably more than either of you. Who was the first one here? And! I'm not the one who was gone into the afternoon and then taking breaks to run off and deliver food and whatever the hell else you were gone doing," Adrian chimes in with a scoff, looking more and more pissy as time goes on and sweat builds on his brow.

"No, that's right, you just ran off with your panties in a wad. Huh, asshole?" A sputtered cough gets caught in my throat, my shoulders folding in as I bang my fist over my chest. That definitely pulls a wide-eyed hoarse laugh from me, taking me completely off guard. He doesn't normally say shit like that. He's always grounded, level-headed, pack lead Cald. He must be feeling the stress of our divide more than he realizes, or more than he's letting on, with Adrian's reaction to us finally finding our mate. Speaking of my mate... I'm *really* over this. I'd much rather be curled around her, playing with her pretty hair. I hope she's doing okay.

Adrian stares us both down, clenching hard enough to crush that crown of his into dust, before shaking his head, tongue in cheek.

"Apt description, Calder. Truly...apt," I add helpfully, golf-clapping and sporting a real special kind of grin aimed at alphahole patient zero. Dirt sprinkles from the bottoms of my boots as I straighten out my legs, knocking them together a few times. I can practically feel the ground shake with tremors as the volcano gets ready to blow. Antagonizing him probably wasn't the best move. I'm being a dick. Regret starts seeping in...until he opens his fucking mouth.

"Yeah? Least I'm not omega-pussy whipped twenty-four hours in." My grin slips, heat and tension rising through my neck and onto my cheeks. That just pisses me off. Which, honestly, might have been his actual goal. Adrian's past teasing. I can't stand him hinting at things about my omega. I don't want him so much as thinking of her if this is how he really feels. Vitriol builds in my throat and vibrates under my skin. Only, I realize with a look from my lead, it's a growl I'm emitting. I just shake my head, trying to clear it of any aggressive fog his words triggered. I'll spare him the hate that wants to spew out, listening to Calder just sigh in frustration. None of us want to be here right now.

"Sage, if you're done stirring up shit, will you get your ass off that bucket before it breaks and come help me finish this?"

"Mmm.... One: I'm good over here. Too cute for a black eye, and you both seem extra moody. And two: I wasn't the one making a dig at his man-panties." Although I do still stand up and make my way over to them. Damn, now I'm the one bickering, too, huh?

"Fine. Jesus christ." Calder stops what he's doing, sitting back on his haunches and bounces whatever piece of metal that's in his hands into his palm, considering. "Adrian, look man, we're here for you. Don't push us away. At some point, you're going to have to face this, and when you do, we'll be here for you. For both you and Opaline. She's just a person, Adrian. A sweet, genuine, kind...person." Not omega, person. I notice his choice of words.

"I'm not doing this again. Don't *push* me, Calder. Just because you two, three, whatever the fuck, want to drop everything and play house with some stray doesn't mean I'll join in."

"...What the fuck did you just say?" I stretch to my full height, head tilting in a primal, animalistic move inherited from my ancestors. My alpha snaps to the surface, my constant leash quickly fraying to shreds at the clear challenge. Breeze hits my teeth as my lips pull back in a silent snarl, fists clenching.

Across from me, my packmate's shoulders bunch, chin lowering and preemptively protecting his neck, meeting me step for step. His white knuckles gripping the shovel in his hands is clear, even from here.

Thick tension builds to breaking as seconds pass and my muscles tense, readying to pounce.

"ENOUGH." Calder's bark booms between the three of us as he stands, towering, harnessing whatever mystical power he somehow holds as a natural pack lead. "You're fucking done Adrian. Walk away, now, before you say something you'll regret."

Adrian's half-feral gaze shoots back to him for a second, locked in a staring contest before he finally submits. Dirt and grass flies as he stubbornly slams the shovel into the ground between him and Calder before stomping off with rigid shoulders.

My eyes widen, my primal taking the backseat again. Calder's jaw is ticking clear as day from here. Proof that he's not immune to our packmate's behavior is mildly comforting to my own uncharacteristic outburst.

"Did he choke down some XL-Asshole pills today? Jesus!" I say with a scowl. "What the fuck is wrong with him!" I snarl. "You can't sit here and tell me that you don't fucki—"

Calder watches our packmate walk away before interrupting my spiral. "Be patient with him, Sage. I feel the same way you do about it. But we haven't been through what he has. That omega will be the best thing that's ever happened to him, if he's able to open himself up even a little bit."

I want to believe that. Adrian is rough around the edges at times, but he's an amazing person and an even better packmate. Truly, he is. The partner he could be for Opaline would be beautiful to witness. He deserves all the happiness in the world. I just fear he won't ever get to the place of acceptance. And, eventually, that will only tear all of us apart, whether Calder wants to admit it yet or not.

Just like that, lava and hot ash rains like it's Pompeii.

We're finishing loading up our supplies into one of the trucks when my ears hone in on two feminine voices carrying in the wind, a bit of a distance away. Perking up, I shield my eyes with a hand until I see my girl come around the corner of the clubhouse. And, damn if the wind isn't knocked out of me.

Her deep red hair shines in the sunlight, catching the slight breeze. She's looking around, and I hope she loves it here as much as we do.

Hot damn, she looks good in my clothes. My alpha pushes me forward, the bulge in my pants growing at the sight before me the further I make my way towards the two of them. Finally, Opaline sees me, and a smile lights her face up as I reach for her, pulling her against me and spinning her around. "There's my princess." I press noisy kisses to her cheeks and temples, setting her back on her feet. Calder's right behind me and takes over before my hands are even off her sides.

"Hey, babygirl." He surprises me a little, picking her up and wrapping her around his waist. The tenderness with which he treats her makes me smile. For a big, intimidating man, I've never seen him quite as soft as he is with her. I'm glad he's loosening the reins on his caution when it comes to her, though. His alpha seems to be quickly settling more, too.

"Thanks for taking good care of our girl, AB!" I smile at the beta and nudge my chin in thanks.

"Oh, absolutely, Sage! I'm more than happy to help with anything else you guys need. We had a great time!" That makes me happy. Good. I was hoping they'd hit it off. We're happy to be Opaline's pack, more than. But, she needs a sense of community too; friends and other people she can talk to. We can't isolate her just to ourselves, even if our alphas want her tucked away in our nest, safe.

"Sure thing, see ya soon." I glance at Annabelle before focusing back on the sweet omega between me and my pack lead.

"Oh, we didn't quite finish the t—"

"No worries, AB, we've got it from here." She might say something else, but honestly, I don't really listen. Her voice just kind of floats away without registering.

Calder tucks a few pieces of wild hair behind her ear and pulls the bottom hem of her shirt down. "Did you not finish the tour?" She shakes her head with a murmured 'no', and Cald glances at me, a few unspoken words shared between us. "Hmm. How about Sage takes over?" he asks, setting her upright on her feet. Yep, I like that idea. Any more time I get to have her near me, I am on board with and would jump over the side.

"Okay!" Her pale green eyes sparkle in excitement.

"I'll leave you two to it then."

"Wait, you're not coming?"

"Sorry, I can't. But I'll see you real soon, little omega." I damn near clench my chest when he winks; the big bastard actually fucking winks.

"Get the hell out of here, you damn alien!"

"What?" Calder tilts his head a little my direction, his confusion clear. Instead of explaining, I grab Opal's hand and pull her to start running with me.

"Skinwalker!"

"... What?"

"Run, sweetheart!" Her giggles and quizzical words chase after me. I swear I can feel Calder's puzzlement and annoyance on my back.

22

Sage

I slow down a bit, looking to see that Calder's already inside and starting the truck.

Opaline's laugh trails behind, her hand warm in mine, and damn it if it isn't the best sound in the fucking world. "Come on," I shoot a grin over my shoulder at her, slowing to a walk.

"Why did we run away like that!" she asks a bit breathlessly. I pull her towards me, ducking us around the side of the clubhouse, behind the huge stack of firewood. We're essentially in a faux alcove, shaded from the sun and prying eyes.

"I was teasing Calder with how gone he is, over you." Her beautiful green eyes stare back at me before dipping away in a shy gesture, the pink that tints her cheeks visible even in the shade. I hum my appreciation, tracing every inch of her glowing face. "You're such a good girl, aren't you, omega?" I ask in a whisper. "Our sweet girl. I can't believe how lucky we are to have found you."

It takes less than two seconds for the flare of her perfume to hit me, my alpha immediately fighting me for control, muscles tensing. Fuck. I put a wet blanket on the growl that starts to echo from deep in me, stepping closer, watching as she follows my lead and steps back. My inner primal tracks everything: her steps, her chest rising and falling, the hands reaching for purchase behind her. With a final step, she hits the wall of the clubhouse, and I position my hand behind her head to stop her from bumping it. "Mmm. Did you like that, sweetheart?" I tease a little, gripping her chin.

The nod is subtle, but the fresh wave of floral honey and brown sugar isn't, hitting me like a tsunami. I want to drown in it, drown in her.

"Yeah? Was it the... *sweet girl* part?" I ask, smirking, tracing my fingers down her chin, neck, to her collarbone and skin peeking through the material of the shirt she's wearing.

She shakes her head, and I feel the smile that stretches my lips.

"Was it maybe... the other part, princess?" Hmm?" I press a gentle kiss to her lips and make my way south, leaving messy marks with my tongue and lips.

The whine she releases snaps something in me, and I pull her up, wrapping her legs around my waist. I'm finally exactly where I've been dreaming of; between her perfect fucking thighs. The heat from her cunt is nearly blinding, all thoughts other than *rut, bite, claim,* coming to a halt. I close my eyes and shake my head a little to clear it and get my shit together, fighting the haze. "My... *good... girl...*" I emphasize each word with a kiss, pressing my cock against her core to ease some of the tension snaking up my spine. "Hmm?"

She nods, her head tilted back to meet my eyes, and I realize her pupils are blown. I'm sure mine don't look much different.

"Say it, omega," I growl, low and guttural at the sight before me, voice nearly unrecognizable. God, she's perfect. I couldn't have begged the stars for a more perfect mate.

"Yes." She says it in a low whisper, but it's like she's trying to gasp for air at the same time.

I use my hips to pin her against the wall fully, freeing both hands to dance over the skin under her top. Obsessed with every inch of her, I watch, entranced, and finally truly see her expression. Pausing, my brows furrow, going on alert, as she looks...pained.

Fuck.

I can't believe I didn't realize this sooner. The flushed and damp skin, big pupils, her perfume, how utterly molten her skin is. She's having a heat spike. She has to be. No wonder I'm fighting my alpha so hard for fucking control right now; everything in me is screaming to claim and breed her. I groan and close my eyes, placing a hand against the wall to steady myself at the thought of her dripping and full of my come. "Jesus christ." I release a breath and try to force down the urges running through every inch of me. "Sweetheart, I think you're having a little bit of a heat spike."

"Yeah..." she trails off, swallowing deeply, fingers twisting my shirt in a death grip. Her tiny hands are practically white and pink, trembling from the effort.

"I've got you, omega. I've got you. You're safe." I bend down and try to kiss her gently. But it quickly turns frantic, the heat coming back to boil all too fast. I pull away, and she whimpers, trying to chase my mouth. "You want me to help you feel better?" I ask. "Make this delicious little pussy feel better?" *Fuck.* As soon as the words leave my mouth, I clench my teeth, kicking myself. I have to fucking get a grip. The last thing I want to do is make her uncomfortable.

"Yes," she whines. "Yes, please. Please, Sage."

"You're sure?" I ask, a little in disbelief. I'm not sure what I was expecting. In fairness, I'm not capable of thinking totally clearly right now with my mate in pain, in a heat spike, and surrounding me with her addictive scent.

"Need you." She tosses her head back against the rough building wall, chest rising and falling quickly, the hair around her face dampened with sweat. "Please..." Her tiny voice sounds so unsure, unconfident. Nope, don't like that one bit.

"I'll always take care of you, Opaline. Always."

I press against her probably a little too hard, devouring her lips in an all-consuming kiss, leaving her no room to ever doubt. She gasps as I press into her, our bodies aligned, and rock my hips. God damn it, fully-clothed dry humping should not feel this fucking phenomenal. "That's it," I groan, the action reminiscent of my teen years.

My mouth crashes back into hers, heat and hunger, her body arching against mine. Fire licks my skin with the sounds she's producing, her omega calling deep to my alpha.

I rock against her, savoring every second, trying to resist the explosion just under the surface. One of her hands grips the back of my neck, the other at the base of my skull in my hair. She pulls her perfect lips away from mine, shining, and drags her mouth to my neck, nosing at my scent gland like it's her only source of oxygen.

"Good girl," I rasp close to her ear. "You're doing so fucking good for me, little omega."

She cries out, the sound muffled against my shoulder, and I feel the wave hit her, her scent somehow flooding me even harder. Her thighs tense, body clenching, hips chasing my own. I don't even try to stop the heat at the base of my spine from pushing out of me, my own groans and snarls dancing with hers as I find my own release too.

I keep grinding and pushing, not stopping until I feel her breath catch and her knees loosen, body melting against mine.

For a moment, the only sound past my thumping heart is our breath, each of us pulling in air. I vaguely realize I absolutely just came in my fucking pants. Must be the happy love-sick hormone high because I kind of don't care. I rest my forehead against hers and take my time memorizing everything about her. How she feels wrapped around me, her residual quiet whimpers of pleasure, the softness of her skin and hair, and the scent I want permanently glued into my nose.

"My sweet omega..." I pepper her face with kisses, taking another few moments in comfortable silence, petting any skin I can get my hands on.

I realize I need to probably fill Calder in on our girl's heat spike. Shit. A list of too many questions build in my mind with zero mental formatting, just chaos.

"How are you feeling?" I ask, pulling away to scan her face and upper body. She looks beautiful in the glowy way women do after they've been pleasured, and overall seems more herself. I feel more in control, too.

"I feel better. It kind of came out of nowhere. I'm sorry." I playfully growl at her for apologizing before she continues. "I thought I was just overheated from touring the indoor hot springs. I didn't realize...it was the beginning of a spike." She traps her bottom lip under her teeth, her brows furrowing a bit, considering something.

"Did the Omega Care Facility have you on suppressants?"

"They did, yeah. We were all on them. Essentially, all omegas pair with packs within three years, the bulk of which happens within the first three to eight months of being there. They probably assume suppressants will hold over our heats until we find mates and move on. They're not really something meant to be taken for a decade." She winces a little, her cheeks turning pinker again. "But, I was able to get them to supply me with enough to last me a couple of months before leaving." She shakes her head, as if thinking. "I'm not sure what's happening. Maybe they're less effective if taken long term?"

"Maybe..." My lips tilt up at one side, pretty sure I already know the answer. "Or, it could be that your omega knows she's safe and she's found her mates." I stroke her cheek, and the smile she gives me nearly stops my heart.

"Yeah..." she sighs, closing her eyes and smiling softly. I hope she likes that thought as much as I do.

"Yeah," I echo.

23

Opaline

After a slew of more questions from Sage, he finally releases me and sets me down so we can finish our tour.

The fact that this is my new home hasn't quite fully sank in yet. I just can't comprehend that it's a real place and not a movie set. In addition to the indoor springs, staff lodging, and main lodging, there is a clubhouse with a snack food selection and a small menu of hot meals available for guests and staff. There are also tables for dining, work stations, and areas for socializing. The interior is similar to others with natural stone, wood, but a bit of brighter lighting overhead. The smell of the open grill and seasoned meats floats through the space.

It's a relief to know that I have options and won't always need to rely on my alphas to provide food for me. The very idea makes me feel a little helpless again, not knowing where or how to locate food yet. The fact of the matter is, this is a completely new town. I don't have transportation and don't know how close a grocery store or eatery is. So, knowing this is here on-site is a huge relief. With everything they've done for me already, I can't stomach adding 'keep the omega fed' to the list.

Sage also takes me through the venue they have available for people to rent out on the property. It was implied prior, but it turns out that Annabelle is their Events Manager. So she handles all of the weddings, birthday parties, etc. that are organized here. He made it sound pretty important and a big source of their income. I hate to admit it because it just makes me sound even more pathetic, but I was hoping she wasn't an integral part of the team here. I haven't mentioned anything to him, either, about my time with Annabelle. There really is no point, and the fact that I'm spending so much time thinking more about it, is embarrassing. It is also far from my right as their omega to be upset that they have past lovers. Or, whatever role it was she or her best friend played in their lives. Surely, if there were still feelings, the guys would tell me? I try to swallow down the thought.

The venue is absolutely breathtaking, as is everything on the resort property. It sits at a slightly higher elevation with sides that can open up completely, turning it into an indoor-outdoor space. The view of the mountains in the distance is something you'd see only on a postcard or in a magazine. The venue gives nearly three-sixty views of the lush surrounding areas. To me, the biggest selling point is the lighting, though, which seems silly. But, the ceiling of the event space is a deep, rich, rough wood with an enormous chandelier in the center with endless rows and rows of multi-size string lighting hanging at various heights across the entire length of the vaulted reception hall. It reminds me of the night sky lit with stars. Sage had mentioned that a lot of the wedding photos would be taken near dusk, in the golden hour, as the sun sets, when the mountains glow. I can just imagine a beautiful pack, or couple, in their fine attire, sharing moments under the sea of lighting, the rainbow of oranges and pinks forming the backdrop of one of the biggest celebrations of their lives. It's beyond clear why the waitlist is as extensive as he explained.

Outside of those buildings, there is also the spa, a massive area of outdoor hot springs, and the courtyard connecting most of the buildings in the center, with various adjoining paths.

The outdoor hot springs sit in the southwest portion of the resort, claiming a massive chunk of the land. Small, rocky pools of steaming water sit nearly layered, carved into the landscape of a foothill, with walking paths dividing them into groups. Sage had explained the formations were mostly natural, with the rock croppings and circular pools forming on their own over thousands of years. They had just taken what nature and the previous owners had built for them and added more cut rocks and pebbles, breaking up the spaces further. It allowed for a more cohesive structure as a whole. They built out the paths for access, and added several waterfalls throughout. Some are even partially secluded behind rock formations, others open to the view of the mountains in the distance. Birds chirping and the sound of tree branches and leaves flowing with the breeze blend with the waterfalls. Everything about this place puts my body at ease. It feels unexpectedly good to be this close to nature.

It's all a little surreal.

Towards the end of our time together, Sage's strong, warm arms wrap around me, surrounding me from behind. He rests his chin near my ear, head bent, soft and even breaths soothing as we slightly sway, wrapped together. We don't speak much. Just hold onto one another, enjoying where we are and appreciating the sounds around us joining in the majesty of the mountain range. Waves of contentment radiate from him with every happy sigh and little squeeze of his arms, his happiness to simply be here with me putting me even more at ease.

Slowly, a smile paints itself onto my face with a wash of emotion. The forgotten, buried part of me that used to doodle hearts and dream of great love starts to stir awake with curiosity and hope, the longer his warmth seeps in and relaxes me.

I can't help but open myself up a little more to the possible life and love story we might build together. The dream I had given up on.

"Don't worry, princess. I'll see you soon," Sage says with a smile. "Plus, something tells me you're going to have a pretty good night."

I quirk an eyebrow at him, studying his face. "And what does that mean?" I laugh a little, still half cuddle-drunk from his warm touches.

"Just a feeling." He winks, and my lower belly heats at the sight. He closes his eyes, groaning, and grabs my hips.

"Sweetheart, if you keep perfuming like that, my alpha isn't going to let me leave you here." Biting his bottom lip with a slight shake of his head, he bends down pressing his mouth to mine, pushing for entrance with his tongue. The kiss is sensual but short-lived, a little to my disappointment. "Fuck. I should go." He traces his thumb over my cheek and jaw, his hand around the side of my neck. "I had such a great time getting to spend time with you today, Opaline. Thank you."

"Me too," I answer truthfully.

"Have a good night, omega." He drops his hand from my neck, and I nearly have to fight my omega's whimper that wants to come out at the loss of contact from our unexpectedly sweet, charming, hunk of an alpha.

Watching Sage turn the corner to the main entrance, I step into my new room, shutting the door, and gasp. There, sitting on my bed, is a beautiful dress, white shoes, a pink leather jacket, and a folded piece of paper with my name on it. "Oh my god..." How did they do this? I don't understand when they could have possibly had time. Rushing forward for the note, my eyes bounce to the bottom, seeing Calder's signature. Reading the few sentences he's scribbled, it reads:

"My sweet omega, please do me the honor of allowing me to take you on a date. I can't wait another moment to officially begin our courting. I hope you like the outfit... I picked something I'd love to see you in. Meet me at the main entrance of your building at six o'clock, should you agree to our courting proposal.

Your alpha, Calder."

I can't help it, I stare at the note, the flow of his handwriting, his signature that is, without reason, exactly and entirely Calder. This is what I have always wanted. And it's being presented to me after all of these years. The pressure and heat that builds behind my eyes is overwhelming, but, in the most beautiful way. Signed... *'Your alpha, Calder.'*

My alpha.

24

Opaline

Practically skipping around the corner, I enter the attached bathroom. Stretching my hand past the curtain of the small shower to turn on the water, I come to a halt, eyes roaming, as water droplets breaking free from their quickly warming stream land on my skin. My inner omega is practically howling in joy.

Calder and Sage put in shelves, stocked with everything I could possibly dream of having for a shower. There's also a gentle, crisp lavender scent floating through the confined space. Looking around, I notice there are small, glittering pucks in the corners releasing the aroma. Taking a deeper breath, I hum in pleasure. Lavender and chamomile have always felt soothing, but now, oddly, the smell also reminds me of Remi's bonded omega, too, which is just another comforting bonus. Calder's mom, I realize with raised brows...

With my omega bouncing and pushing for me to dive into our gifts, I can't resist. My fingers land and linger on every single product: sleek white bottles labeled in elegant script, mint colored jars of shower jellies, gels, scrubs, and hair masks. I can't believe they did this. Even with the maintenance issue they were dealing with, having their hands full, they still found time to do this huge gesture for me, to gather each of these items, and set everything up, perfectly faced and aligned like in an expensive store.

Taking a step back, my palms land on the small sink, my attention snapping to the mirror above it. Steam is already starting to fog the edges of the reflective glass. Meeting my own eye, it's nearly like seeing someone else. Not in the scary dissociative derealization way that had started haunting me in recent weeks. Not even the prior version of me. Certainly not the most recent version of me. But, instead a new version. A happy, glowing, smiling version.

Almost missing it, my hand grazes the corner of something, catching my attention. There's a second note placed on the counter. Plucking it up, I bite my lip, bursting with excitement. *"You deserve a little pampering. Since we can't be there to constantly spoil you (yet), please spoil yourself. Enjoy, omega."*

His words jump off the smooth paper the more times I read them, tightening my throat. The thought of being so cared for, after everything... It's overwhelming, and these little moments keep hitting in waves as I find my footing. I can't help it. It's not the luxury products, clothes, or even the dinner they've given me. It's that all of this shows me how much they're paying attention, tuned into my needs and even the wants of my omega. The realization frankly leaves a vulnerable knot in my stomach. It's my dream to be treated like a princess, to find my mates...but why does it also leave me with a sense of unease?

No one has done anything even close to this, a kind gesture like this, since my mom died. There's so much unspoken intention and care. Looking back between the note and the lovely gifts sitting perfectly in the shower, it feels like too much. It's more than each of these things individually. It's their combined attention, intention, the gifts, and a space to finally breathe and recover that's being handed to me.

Closing my eyes, I feel the full spectrum of the emotion about to pull me in from a safe shore. I let myself feel and lean into it all until I land back on happiness, opening to see a sheen in my eyes, tear tracks, and a smile back in place.

The squeal that slips free as happiness again raises within me, gripping the note to my chest, would be embarrassing if anyone were to hear me. Courting gifts aren't just an old tradition passed down. They're a tangible way for alphas to show their devotion and interest. Offerings meant to prove they can and will provide for me, as their omega. And, as materialistic and selfish as it may seem to some, the biology of omegas drives our craving for their courting gifts and the show of their ability. It isn't always material things. But, selfish or not, omegas are wired to desire this kind of care; the instinctual need to be claimed and cherished.

And *our* courting had officially begun. With the sweetest, dreamiest declaration from my scent matches.

There's a twinge in the back of my mind, though. The two mystery packmates, Everette and Adrian. Statistically, there is a strong chance they'd be my scent matches too. That's been its own little box in the back of my head I haven't processed yet. Sage had explained that Everette is away on a trip and unfortunately won't be able to be in contact, despite their efforts calling the retreat's management team. My inner omega can't fathom how this can't possibly be important enough for them to interrupt his ocean-side yoga, sound bath, meditation retreat. I, on the other hand, am trying to be logical, though.

Even as my omega's small insecurity and annoyance lingers, a bigger part of me feels...relieved. Simultaneously, a part of me is happy to have this time with just Calder and Sage. There's been so much change so quickly. I need time with each of them, but also frankly need time by myself outside of survival mode and scarcity mindset. It isn't that I don't want to meet them. That couldn't be further from the truth. It's just all already so much. Calder, Sage, and the heat spike, on top of moving and relearning a new location. Everything that felt familiar to me is gone, suddenly. Everything feels like it's both raveling and unraveling so fast, I haven't had time to just feel into it all. Not like I really need to in order to feel grounded in reality.

I need this time. With Calder, who gives me hope and offers a steady support. With Sage, who's bewilderedly reawakening an old, playful part of me. But yes, with myself, alone, too. Time to feel something other than fear, panic, or anxiety. I've been in survival mode and forgot what it feels like to just simply...be. To sit in the stillness of a moment and not have to plan my next steps, meal, or even the next way to protect myself.

The future with Everette and Adrian would unfold as the stars intended. I don't even know what they look like. I only have brief descriptions or mentions that they've given me, thus far.

The excitement they have for me to meet Everette is palpable. He sounds like a down-to-earth, creative, intelligent alpha with a loving, gooey center. I imagine him to be like one of the alphas in movies that make you smile and cry watching him fall in love, kissing his mate under a pouring rain, on screen. Admittedly, thoughts of him make me a little nervous.

Not in a bad, frightening way. Nearly the opposite. In an anticipatory, what-if-I'm-not-good-enough way. Each of these men seem to have traits that call to myself and my omega. But something about Everette seems almost healing, just at the thought of him.

Adrian... I have somehow managed to learn even less about. Just the couple of sentences from Calder's lips. The silence surrounding his name feels almost secretive, whether it is or isn't, and I can't say I care for it. I want more, want to learn as much as I can to know what to expect. All the blank space just leaves my mind to wonder and fill the curious void with less-than-stellar images.

Overall though, I don't know if the depth of what I'm already feeling so strongly for Sage and Calder is my primal's instinct, genuine attraction, or just the pathetic need to belong to someone so badly I'll cling to any inclination or scrap of love and care thrown my way.

Maybe that's part of the unease I feel flickering to life now and then.

25

Calder

Sage's bark of a laugh spears through my bedroom and into the closet I'm currently standing in. Brows furrowed, I peek around the corner to see what he's laughing so hard at.

"Omega Courting 101? First date ideas? Oh my god... *How to impress your omega?* Calder!" Damn it all to hell. Gritting my teeth, I stomp into the room to see him sitting on my bed, face illuminated by the small screen. "I'm— hey!" Snatching my phone from his grip, I roll my eyes as he flops dramatically onto his back in what could only be described as heinous laughter.

Stepping back into my walk-in closet, I check the mirror and groan, unbuttoning the third shirt I've tried on. I want to make a good impression for our first date. Not just that, but the start of our courtship, should she agree. That train of thought nearly knocks me on my ass. The fact that she might not show. Might not want this as desperately as both Sage and I. Rubbing my chest at the thought, I swallow and finger through the same row of shirts I've been staring at for the last hour. None of them feel good enough. It's a lot of pressure for a shirt.

"You're hilarious," Sage comments with a groan, laughter lingering in his voice. "It's cute, though. I mean it. I've never seen this side of you. All disheveled-like. Picking out clothes like it's the first day of school."

"Are you here just to mock me? Because you can leave. I didn't ask you to be here." I sigh in frustration.

"I know. I'm sorry, I'm sorry. I really do like seeing you two together. She brings out a new side of you. It suits you. Just jealous you get first date by yourself." I can hear the pout hiding in his voice, which tells me there is probably a little truth to his jealousy. Since he'd spent the entire afternoon with her, we'd decided a solo date for Opal and I would be best. And although we may not be privy to partake in all the traditionalist's ideals, it is customary to start the courtship with the pack's lead alpha. "Just thought it'd be both of us for our first date. I don't know. What the hell am I going to do tonight without her..." he trails off.

Stepping back out of the closet, I try another shirt, pulling the sides forward to close the line of buttons on the front. "She needs slow," I murmur, half paying attention. I hope this damn shirt doesn't scream trying too hard. Fuck, does it? Is black too severe?

Sage screeches a god-awful, high-pitched sound I wouldn't think him capable of, in response. "I can do slow!"

Says the man who very literally cannot, in fact, do anything slowly. I raise an eyebrow at him soundlessly. It has its desired effect, and he just shrugs, blowing air through his lips, and sits up in bed. Before turning back around, I notice the pants he has on and growl a little. "Damn it, Sage, did you wear those clothes outside?"

"Yep."

"Get the hell out of my bed then!" Jesus christ. If any part of him is here to be helpful, he's having the exact opposite affect.

"Our omega's dried come and slick is still on me. I'm not taking them off." Fuck. I could scent her on him, but I just assumed it was residual from him helping her through the heat spike. I didn't consider the fact...

I genuinely can't help the half groan, half growl that escapes me at the thought, swiping my hand over my face and through my hair in a poor attempt at concealing my reaction. "That's what I thought," he adds smugly. "I could, uh, roll around a bit, ya know? Yeah?"

"I swear to god, Sage," I sigh in defeat. "Can you please leave already?"

"Nah, I like it in here. Energy feels better." He shrugs again, but I notice something heavy in his gaze as he glances away and grabs a bicep with his hand, rubbing up and down. Seemingly almost self-soothing.

"Hey," I whisper. Stepping closer to him, I grip his shoulder, getting his full attention. "What's going on? What are you thinking about?"

Pushing his fingers through his dark roots, he grips the ends of his hair, the slight curls straightening from the strain. "You're not upset with me, about earlier, are you? It was intense. My primal was hit hard with her perfuming. I just hope I handled it right."

The uncertainty in his eyes guts me. Sitting down so we're nearly at eye level, I pat his knee. "You did exactly what I would hope you would. You took care of our omega, exactly as she needed. She was in pain, in a spike, and it would have lasted hours had you not taken care of her. I could never be upset about that, at you." I shake my head. "You hear me?"

His lips twitch a little to one side, the light returning to his eyes. "Yeah. Thanks, man." Nodding, I stand up and smooth down the front of my shirt. "So, what time are you picking her up?" He sighs, expelling any residual insecurity.

Ducking my head to the side a little, I turn and head into the bathroom. "Six," I mutter.

"Huh?"

"Six..."

"Calder, you still have an entire hour! Oh my god!" His laugh echoes through the space so loudly I slam the bathroom door shut with a grumbled curse. Looking in the mirror, I see the pink on my cheeks, and I'm thankful for the small mercy that he didn't notice.

I stand outside the staff quarters' entrance for longer than I need to. Longer than I probably should. If it were literally anyone else, people would undoubtedly be suspicious of what the hell I'm doing pacing back and forth on the small patio muttering to myself with ridiculous hand gestures. That knowledge is far from lost on me. Yet here I am, heavy boots carving into the concrete, their repetitive thumps and grating turns all I can focus on past the noise in my head.

Releasing a deep breath, I try to give myself a little internal pep-talk, further effort in forgetting the grimace of one of our seasonal employees as he snuck by me in an awkward shuffle between the two of us. I give myself a reminder that I can do this. I can give her an enjoyable evening and be a good representation of our pack and what our future can ultimately look like together. While also not being overbearing or too aloof. I can be the exact right amount of obsessive. *Shit, no, not obsessive. Interested.* I can be funny and charming, right? Her perfect mate? I can be that. This is starting to spiral...

"Hi." *Shit.* I'm so in my head that I don't even hear the main door quietly open behind me. The soft, sweet, feminine sound reaches me, and without a single doubt, I know it's Opaline. Snapping my attention to her, her presence is overwhelming, and I freeze at the sight of her, jaw going slack. *Double shit.*

She's here. Really here. Which means, she wants us to court her.

"Hi, sweet omega." I regain consciousness and take an eager step toward her with my hand out, an invitation for her touch and her hand in mine. "You look beautiful. Breathtaking." She does. There aren't words to properly describe her beauty. Her hair's shinier, and her skin now practically glowing. She's just radiating happiness, and god, it feels good to witness. Especially knowing she's had several solid meals now, plenty of rest, and the space to properly cater to her inner omega's whims. Like pampering herself before our date. With less hesitation than I'm honestly expecting, she places her tiny fingers in my palm, a soft smile on her face.

"Thank you." I'm utterly entranced watching her move closer. Every bit of her is a dream. So much so that I understand her prior urge to pinch herself to confirm this is all real. If she suddenly evaporated into a glittering haze, I can't say I'd be fully surprised.

"Come here, babygirl." The urge to hold her close and mark her with my scent for all to know she's claimed is undeniable. Already, as time passes, the fire under my skin grows restless, and I know the agitation won't ease up until she's in my arms with my scent on her, and hers on mine.

She melts into my touch, and in an instant, I feel more settled. All it took, apparently, was having her close to me to feel peace and get out of my head. The mind chatter, in retrospect, was entirely unnecessary. Based on her body language and extra sweet hint of her scent, I can safely assume that she feels more relaxed, too. Having her against me this close feeds a primal part of me, but there's still an unrelenting desire to be even closer.

With each fresh inhale, taking in her wild floral scent, the instinct and urge I couldn't name just seconds ago is all too clear.

I want us to be as connected as we can be, long to be buried inside her. I can't tell if it's me or my primal driving my thoughts as my alpha pushes for dominance, just at the mere flash of an image of her crying out in pleasure under me, coming around my cock, knot deep.

Swallowing deeply in an effort to smother the growl rising quickly, and with all the willpower the stars have blessed me with, I push the thoughts down.

Fuck. I don't know if she can sense where my thoughts have moved, but I get a burst of her perfume, and it's nearly my undoing. It isn't typical for alphas to produce perfume, like omegas, but for scent-matches, I try to recall if maybe it's different. Maybe my scent has just as much effect on her as hers does on me.

Pulling back and regaining control, I press my lips to her temple and release the hold I have her in. The loss of contact feels all wrong, like I'm suddenly missing my newly sewn-in extra limb. The sensation makes no sense, but that's exactly how it feels. The need to cling to her is uncomfortably strong. I wonder if maybe our fated souls were once connected as stardust, and coming to life at being so close again, urging to be rejoined. It's a beautiful thought. I want us permanently chest to chest, her frame wrapped around me. "Come on, omega." My voice vibrates with a slight residual grit, but she doesn't seem concerned at all. Her smile is still in place and transformative as ever. "The night is young."

26

Opaline

Calder and I stroll, hand in hand, through the small town just a short drive from their springs resort. Every single thing about this place is perfect, like a fairytale. I can't get over how much I enjoy just being here, with him. The air's crisp, carrying the lingering scents of cakes and sweets from a nearby bakery, grilled food from a couple of outdoor food trucks, and even the natural pine and fir from the trees that frame the hills that tower around us.

Glowing string lights curl around uniquely crafted lamp posts and frame the windows of nearly every storefront we pass. The shops, restaurants, and little stores are painted in pastels with flower boxes and chalkboard signs along the way. Saying I love it here is a severe understatement.

But, to be honest, I can't help but wonder if part of the reason why is simply due to the man beside me, not the charming town. The steadiness and warmth he exudes leaves me with a constant feeling of safety I've been missing. Just being in his presence gives me a sense of peace I wasn't expecting so soon, not with the scarce interactions we've had so far. But that's exactly what Calder seems to be: steady, warm, and safe.

"Hey, umm," I stop walking, stepping to the side of the walkway even though it's empty. Calder's hand still in mine, I trace my thumb over the top of his hand, the thick veins standing out and catching my eye. "I just want to say thank you, for tonight, and just everything, really."

He chuckles a little, the sound so deep it draws my omega to stand up straight and proper under his attention. "We haven't even gone in anywhere yet, babygirl."

Heat rises to my cheeks and chest as my hand playfully smacks his bicep without realizing it. To him it probably feels like a bug landing on his skin. "Not that. Well, that too. But...all the little ways you keep checking on me to make sure I'm comfortable and taken care of hasn't gone unnoticed. I really appreciate everything you, and Sage, have done for me and need you to know."

Calder's free hand rubs the back of his neck, almost nervously. He opens and closes his mouth as if not sure what to say back. I study his face and realize there's a twinge of pink to his face and the front of his neck too, I've not yet seen. My big alpha *is* nervous. Or maybe he's not used to being noticed and appreciated. I guess as the lead of their pack, everything, or most everything, falls to him. I hope he's getting the recognition I'm sure he deserves. But if he's not, I can be the one who shows him how wonderful he is. The thought sends a bubble of warmth through me. The urge to soothe his nervous energy sits heavily. I decided earlier that I would allow myself this chance at happiness. The opportunity to dream again about this future I still so badly want. And part of that means following my omega's lead and not fighting her. She told me to trust the strange alpha behind the pub, and look where I am now.

Following my intuition, I slowly stretch my arm up and cup his cheek, tracing my thumb against the freshly shaven skin in what I hope is a soothing gesture for this giant alpha. My eyes linger on different areas: his jawline, bottom lip, hairline, and finally land on his own eyes. The unspeakably stunning golden color reflects the setting sun, and the tiny spots of green in his right eye seem brighter from it. "My precious, perfect omega." His words are a whisper, contrasting his height and god-like frame. The whine that follows is soft and takes me a second to realize it's me making the sound.

It must call to his alpha because in the span of a second, I'm lifted and wrapped around his waist, being carried a handful of feet to the end of the building and into an alley. "Mine." With a hand wrapped around the back of my head, the yellow pastel siding cools my back as his weight settles between my thighs. It's impossible not to fall under his spell of masculinity and strength. Watching the path those golden eyes take between my lips and my own eyes, I put him out of his misery, conflict clear to see. Offering my obvious consent, I lean up and reach my lips towards his with a needy whimper, sliding my palms up his solid chest and around his neck.

It's all he needs before his mouth is crashing into mine, lips soft and obsessive. The growl reverberating from him does nothing to quell the desire and heat building between my thighs. Desperate to deepen our kiss, I open for him, letting his tongue dance against mine in a rhythm that sparks fire in my veins, flowing to the best places. The entire kiss feels like a dichotomy of his natural dominance and gentleness.

"Shit. I'm sorry." He pulls back, too suddenly, putting me down. "God, I'm sorry."

"No, I want it. I want you," I say, more than a little breathless and lightheaded.

Bending and resting his forehead to mine, I can literally feel his smile before seeing it. "You're so perfect. I want to do this right. I want to spoil you a little and spend time with you. Cuddle up while we eat dessert. Let's enjoy the night, okay?" he asks gently.

I haven't been on a real date in a long time, if ever, now that I think of it. Not like the one he's planned for us tonight, with gifts and sweet teasing touches, holding hands, like in the movies. This isn't just a tolerated date to get to the end of the night, and what that meant. Being at the Facility didn't make dating impossible, but it was pretty damn close. Most times I needed to scratch the itch, it ended up in dimly-lit bar bathrooms when I tagged along with other omegas the assigned weekends we were allowed to leave campus.

I know deep down, that's not what tonight is for Calder. A small rush of anxiety rises as a wave of unwanted thoughts tangle, ways I'm not good enough to deserve him or—

His fingers brush mine, and the gentle touch is enough to bring me back to earth.

I'm not still dreaming and wishing for this moment. I'm in it.

Curling my hand in his, I squeeze reassuringly and take my next step, at his side.

27

Calder

Opaline and I hop into a couple of stores along our stroll route, nearly to the end, where the street is closed down. My eyes track everything she touches, almost touches, or hell, even looks at. Those little, slender fingers stop to pet soft things, admiring paintings and jewelry. But not once has she actually picked something up to take with us. She says she doesn't want anything. The weight of my building disappointment feels like rocks being added to a sinking boat every time her fingers drift away from yet another item.

I'm kicking myself seeing that maybe this isn't the romantic idea of a date I thought it'd be. Romance may not exactly be my greatest suite.

The smile stays nearly glued to her face, though, so maybe she is genuinely enjoying herself. Trying to find that balance between overbearing and nonchalant, I give her space and don't push the matter...yet.

As the sun starts to make its way towards the edge of the earth, the glow of pinks and golden red paints everything in an unbelievable aura. It wasn't every night we got showstopping sunsets. This feels a bit like a gift from the universe, a nudging support just for her and me.

We reach the end of the main street of Mount Fir's Landing's downtown. If you can rightfully call it that feels doubtful. Either way, the street's permanently closed with large, concrete, spherical roadblocks that are painted by several local artists and made into huge flowerbeds still bursting with color. But, in addition, the little end-cove has more bulbous string lights crisscrossing from one side of the street to the other. Small metal tables and chairs are placed in the open street, designating the space as a place to relax, socialize, and eat.

She tilts her head up toward the glowing lights strung up across the street, and with the air hovering just out of reach, suddenly I feel like I forget how to breathe. She isn't doing anything special, calling for attention, but hell, everything she does feels special. It's a simple moment of her appreciation for an innocuous bit of beauty. But, no, the weight in my lungs is because she's here with me in real life. No longer the ghost of a concept, or dream woman I wondered if I'd ever get the chance with. The dying golden sun shines over her skin, the various lighting reflecting in her beautiful green eyes further mesmerizing my inner alpha and I, both.

Mine. The primal part of my brain silently snarls the word, pushing for me to claim and sink my teeth into the soft pale flesh of her neck.

Luckily, I've noticed the ability to take control over my alpha is getting a little easier each time we're together. I feel much more collected than during our meet at Rem's, and the thoughts settle quickly.

Clearing my throat, I ask, "Do you like it?" I keep my voice low and hope it comes off as casual as it sounds to me. She turns towards me, somehow her smile just a little bigger.

The moment feels like the world slows, all sound fading as she fills my vision. The image of her glowing red hair in the fiery sunset, and bright green eyes alit with joy is so striking. I have no doubt this will be one of many memories I'm praying we'll get to experience together, that I will never forget, even through my dying breath.

"I love it. It's just so breathtaking. I mean, the sunset, the buildings, the lights...you. It's perfect."

Bending slightly and bringing her hand to my mouth, I press an easy kiss to her skin. "I'm so glad you think so. Because I think so too." The way the words pour out of me, the way my eyes trace her face and hair, I hope to hell she knows I'm not just talking about our surroundings. "Now, omega, you're going to pick out at least one thing from the next three stores. If you let me spoil you a little, then I can guarantee some of the best dessert you've ever had." I raise a brow, lips quirked to the side, waiting.

A playful roll of those gorgeous eyes and quick loss of eye contact tells me I won.

I finally get my sweet omega to loosen up a bit with her silent requests for things as we pop in places. Letting her know she either picks stuff out now, or I come back tomorrow and grab everything she looked at for more than two seconds seemed to do the trick. Now, every time she wants something, it turns into her cute face peeking up at me with her lips pursed, or a shy little movement, like tucking her hair behind her ear. To say I'm thrilled is a gross understatement. It's exactly what I was hoping for. And, damn providing something other than necessities for my omega puffs up my chest enough that I could shoulder the world.

A few bags sway in time with my steps, bunched my hand. She's ended up getting a book, some handcrafted chocolates and candies, a couple of silken nightgowns, and oddly, a postcard. That one surprises me a little bit. I know she doesn't really have family from what my dad had passed along from her own quick explanation. But I just didn't realize she had the opportunity to make many friends. Which is a shitty fucking thought on my end. I don't know who the postcard would be for. Something tells me she'll open up about it when she's ready.

I look over at her as the chime above the door to the little odds and ends store sounds softly behind us. She's starting to lose that little pep in her step, her smile softening, and the times her head rests on my arm is becoming more frequent. "Hey, little omega, you feeling okay?"

Silken, dark strands are smooth under my palm as I stroke her hair as best I can from the angle with her head resting against my bicep, and hands around my forearm. She hums gently, seemingly forcing soft, pliant eyes to mine. "Yeah. I'm sorry, I don't know why I'm just suddenly a little tired. I'm sorry." She pulls away as if ashamed she's done something wrong, looking off to the side.

"Hey, no. Don't apologize for how you're feeling. I don't always pick up on everything." I tug her gently a couple of feet to the side, tucking her against me. "If you're feeling tired, or want to go home, or need food, literally anything, please tell me, babygirl. I will always do everything in my power to make sure you are content and taken care of. Always." The words 'you're my dream come true' linger on my tongue, but just don't feel quite right. I don't know where she's at with our situation herself, and don't want to overwhelm her. Considering that she's wanting time to herself and a little space to live on her own, I don't think blurting out my newly scribbled diary entries towards her would be what she needs.

On top of that, a small part of me wonders if she's needing so much rest and feeling sleepy, is simply because her omega is finally safe and taken care of. I can practically feel my alpha puff up in response, pleased she's comfortable and safe with us. A nod is all I receive in response. "How about this? We walk over to the ice cream shop a couple of stores down and get a little treat. I'll order food to be delivered and take you home. Sound good?"

"I just feel bad you planned this whole night for us to walk around and enjoy the town and have dinner together. And, here I am rui—"

A slow growl interrupts her as she looks up at me with eyes slightly widened and small smile. "Nope. Absolutely not, baby. Don't you dare finish that sentence. You don't *ruin* any god damn thing, ever. Understood?"

"Um, okay." It's a start. I'll spend every waking day I have on this earth with her convincing her she's perfect if that's what it takes.

My lips touch her hairline, and I hold her against me, swaying gently for a few moments, watching her eyes close. I'm torn between making sure she's fed dinner and taking her home so she can rest. "Come on, sweetheart," I whisper, putting a small space between us.

28

Opaline

"You know I can walk, right?" I tease Calder as he holds me wrapped around him, carrying me up the path to the staff lodging. The soft lights in the ground surround and illuminate the walkway with sparkles and a warm golden light flares, every few feet. The sounds of what I assume are crickets or cicadas work together in their symphony to fill the air around us, too.

Calder chuckles in the way I'm starting to love, the sound more of a vibration to be felt than an actual noise. Somehow, he supports all of my weight in one arm and still manages to hold onto the bags and ice cream in the other.

Stepping through the main door, the open communal space is dark and quiet, no one else around to enjoy it at this hour. Heading to the left, down the hallway towards the room they've given me, we reach my door. Calder balances our evening's spoils, entering the four-digit code to open my bedroom door, the keypad lighting up with a flash of green as the soft beep sounds twice.

"Wait, how do you know the code to my room?" I look at him quizzically.

"Each of us has master codes to all of the doors in the resort in case of emergency." Ah, well, that explains a little more about how they were able to get into my room to drop off food for me. I guess I should have assumed that was the case. The urge to tease him about bringing me dinner being an emergency tingles in my being, but I leave it.

He finally sets me down onto my feet next to my bed, and I startle a little, noticing something new sitting atop the small dresser. "Where did that come from?" I ask, eyeing the black screen.

"I had Sage set it up while we were out. Just something small to make sure you're comfortable and enjoying yourself. Plus, he needed a distraction. I'll check to make sure, but he texted to let me know that he set up several channels and added you to our accounts. So you can have something to fall asleep to." His soft eyes peek over at me briefly, and I wonder if he knows that I asked Remi to have the bench seat in his bar so that I could fall asleep to the sound of the TV. I can't believe this man, these men. The fact that they even thought to do this for me is incredible.

"I can't believe you would do that for me. Calder...thank you so much. For everything." I couldn't say those two little words enough for them to comprehend my gratitude.

"Babygirl, believe me when I tell you, we have been waiting a very long time for this. The opportunity to care for our omega. You're the center of our pack." He quickly wipes his hand over his face, shaking his head slightly, a bluster of small movements, as if he's said something wrong. The gestures confuse me a little. "I mean, if you want. No pressure," he adds, looking around, his eyes searching. Oh. I think he is embarrassed? Is that what's happening?

"Calder."

He reaches for the remote sitting on the end of the bed, eyes meeting mine again with a bit of hesitancy.

"I've waited for this for a long time, too," I whisper, his size seemingly taking up the majority of the room, even as he sits. The very idea of sharing this part of me is nerve-wracking, the heaviness of it sinking to my stomach so quickly that I sit down on the fluffy comforter next to him, pulling a pillow into my lap like a sad shield. "I gave up on the idea of ever finding my pack. Honestly, years ago. As more time went on... I just realized it would never happen for me. We were always taught at the facility that omegas were coveted and desired. It was our meaning in life to find our pack and build a life with our alphas."

I smile weakly at the thought, the memories flooding me as I try to fight them back. "I mean, everyone knows that's an omega's life path. Everyone wants to be an omega. Even before I presented, in high school and growing up, every girl dreamed of the day they'd present as one. Of being considered so precious and sought after. After years of not being chosen, not finding matches, so few courtship proposals, I felt like a failure to my designation." Calder abruptly stands, tensing his fists with a scowl, like he's purposefully stopping himself from moving towards me. Collecting me in his arms seems to be a consistent urge of his. One that's quickly becoming addicting. "The fact that I'm being given this chance after all of these years is a lot to fully accept, Calder. To know now, after so long, that I was just waiting for my literal scent matches and that you existed? It's unbelievable and feels a little too good to actually be true. Like the other shoe is just waiting to drop."

I feel the tickle of my tears spilling from the corners of my eyes as they slide down my cheeks. I reach to swipe them away, but before I actually complete the motion, strong arms are finally around me, a huge chest blocking my vision, and soft words murmured to soothe me. "I'm sorry if this isn't how you pictured meeting your omega." I just can't stop. Everything that's been bottled up is overflowing and pouring out of me unbiddenly. "I promise I'm not trying to hurt Sage or you by staying here on the property before moving in with you. Just.." I sigh. "Please, try to understand that this is a lot, and honestly, I'm still a little terrified one day I'll wake up, and it won't be real. I just need a bit of time to reconnect with myself, too. Ugh," I groan. "Sorry, this turned into a cry-fest. I don't know what's going on with me. I'm not normally like this. Anyway, my point is that this is a dream of mine too, Calder. I know I haven't outright said it. But I want you to know it means just as much to me to have this chance with you, Sage, even Everette and Adrian when the time comes."

I take a solid breath, eyes landing on his, and the breath freezes in my lungs. The depth and range of emotion and longing radiate from him in waves, pouring straight from his beautiful golden eyes into me, utterly captivating. This man looks at me like I'd caught a shooting star from the sky and bottled it just for him, like a firefly.

I'm not sure how long, honestly, we gaze into each other's eyes. As time passes and tension builds in the silence, it becomes more and more clear we're done talking. The pull of his alpha to my omega wins in an instant, and we move in sync. Calder's so strong, moving my body and placing me where he wants me feels like it's nothing for him. My legs are forced open from the width of his waist as I straddle his lap, big hands tight on my hips. Our mouths connect with little finesse, being led by nothing more than urgent desire. He consumes me like he wants to memorize the feel of my lips and the taste of my tongue.

I whine with need, and I can feel Calder's alpha fighting him to take control each second his hands get tighter and just a tad more rough in their affections. Fighting to please his omega. He growls so deeply in response to my omega's call, I tremble, the heat in my body surging to the surface, suddenly far too hot to be anywhere near comfortable. My skin flushes like prickles of fire trace my nerves, shooting in every direction. I try and fail with my legs wrapped around him to rub my thighs together. My perfume explodes, slick trickling from between my thighs. "Please, please Calder." I don't know what I'm begging for, but I know I need him to act on the undeniable, quickly burning desire building between our bodies, the sensation akin to lightning readying to strike.

His own scent, coffee, frosted pine, and the distinct feeling after a rainstorm explodes around me. I'm half gone, half out of my mind, and fuzzy with profound need. "My omega. Mine." With one easy, smooth motion, he has me pinned under him. I watch as he closes his eyes and shakes his head slightly as another growl echoes from the depths of his chest and throat. He's fighting his alpha, and damn it if I don't want him to. I want everything he can give me, right this second.

My shaking fingers gently touch his face, the tension in his jaw clear. I call his name and gather his attention. I swear those eyes glow brighter as they look back, tracing my face and landing on my neck. Some distant part of me, behind a bubble in the back of my mind, wonders if he's about to go into a rut. The other part urges me to stretch my neck and give him clear access to bite and claim.

"Alpha," I whimper, forcing myself to return to the reality before me, back to what feels like solid ground. "I'm having another heat spike, I think." It's the only thing that makes sense, that would explain both of our intense reactions only amplified by the other.

He takes a breath as if trying to center himself, too, and goes quickly into reassuring me. "I've got you, little omega. I promise, I've got you."

I nod and feel my shoulders and hips loosen, trusting he absolutely does have me.

"Do you trust me to take care of you?" he asks. The words come out with a cavernous vibration, residual from his alpha trying to take the lead.

"Yes, I do." As soon as I utter the words, I realize they are undoubtedly true. I know my alpha will take care of me. Not just for my heats or heat spikes. But for anything and everything I could need. The thought's cloudy but less foggy than anything running through my brain had been just seconds before.

"My good girl." He says the words with an appreciation like you'd mutter when enjoying your favorite dessert. The teasing tone also makes me one hundred percent positive Sage told him about our little side-quest this afternoon during our tour. Oddly, I'm not embarrassed. Instead, I release a full, genuine laugh that equally floats through the room with my newly perfumed, needier scent.

29

Opaline

Calder's lips turn upward, eyes heavy with lust. Gracefully moving to sit on his haunches next to me, his form appears even more massive from my current vantage, sending chills skittering over my skin. Anyone else, it would feel more than intimidating. Throughout our time together, I've realized he is absolutely close to seven feet tall, but more than that, every single inch of his body is honed like an actual god. It feels like the closest analogy I can think of. I take him in, lingering on spots here and there, finally landing on the very noticeable bulge in his pants.

The urge to lick my lips is a new, foreign instinct, imagining what exactly is underneath and how it might feel inside me. God, just at the thought, I moan and close my eyes, hips wriggling. Warm lips fall to my neck, down my collarbone, and in between the skin showing partially between my breasts from my dress's material dislodging itself in our haste.

Falling into the sensation of every point his tongue and lips touch my skin is like piecing together the outer ring of a puzzle, wanting the final piece to be snapped into place. "God, Calder," I breathe. His moan in response does nothing other than push me further towards the literal edges of my sanity.

Finally, his huge, warm hand teases my inner thigh, his touch light. Not what I need. I whimper in frustration, my chest flushed and on fire. "I've got you, omega. Trust your alpha to take care of you." His tone's soft, but more demanding and dominating than some men think they sound when yelling and shouting their assertion. I try to fall back into that layer of trust, thighs starting to tremble in anticipation.

Fingertips caress the crease between my hip and thigh, searching. "Is my omega not wearing panties?" His growl is enough to make my eyes snap to his, at attention. I shake my head but don't say anything else. I don't think the response of how all of my undies are still dirty and need cleaning would keep the moment as spicy as I want it to stay. "Naughty, aren't you?" *Yes, let's go with that.*

He utters the words just as his fingers land exactly where I want them, on my pussy. Our groans are simultaneous, a duality between femineity and masculinity. Tracing his touch downward, he gathers my slick and presses on my clit experimentally, studying my responses and what seems to make my legs shake or tense. And, god am I shaking. I'm desperate to come, need it, and quickly become a whimpering mess. I can feel the sweat coating my skin, slick pooling between my thighs, the longer he touches and teases, circling the small bud over and over.

Just as a cry, desperate to break free, forms in my throat, he lowers his hand and presses into me in small nudges, until he's seated fully. His fingers are long and huge, like the rest of him, and feel so fucking good my eyes roll back. It's a relief to finally have him inside me, pumping in and out. It only makes me crave his cock and knot. Fresh slick coats his fingers at my dirty thoughts, eliciting a pleased hum. His movements speed up slightly, fingers fucking me like I need, thumb heavily tracing my clit. I do nothing to stop or lessen the encouraging words, whimpers, and begging that fills the small space, tumbling from my lips.

I can feel the tension growing, that part of me spiraling tighter and tighter, closer to the precipice as pleasure overtakes me. As I'm about to go over, the pressure of his thumb's suddenly gone. Before I can scream in protest, his warm, wet tongue takes its place, his lips forming a suction over the spot I need it most.

Stars explode behind my eyelids, and dizziness chases me as more pleasure than my body could possibly hold consumes me. "C-Calder!" His name is a bellowed prayer, my moans following nonsensically and nonstop, mirroring his own appreciative groans as he licks and sucks. My hands fumble blindly, desperate for purchase, reaching and fisting anything they can. His tongue and fingers never stop fucking into me until I spiral a second time, nearly passing out from pleasure, breathless and boneless.

"Oh my god, Calder." I can barely speak, brushing hair from my face and neck with shaking hands. Looking back to my alpha, any other words are lost in translation, half processed by my brain before falling off into a sea of nothingness. His tongue laps at his palm and glistening fingers, cleaning off my come and slick like it's his last meal. Lips parted, I watch with rapt attention, eyes heavy and half dazed.

Glancing back at my still-exposed pussy, his tongue slips out a little against his bottom lip like he wants more, sending me into a residual spasm around nothing. "Fuck," he groans. I feel a little floaty, smiling, and giggle lightly. He glances back up and repositions himself so our faces are more closely aligned. Our lips meet again, the taste of my arousal on his tongue, our scents a combined mess in the confined air. "You have no idea what you do to me, little omega," he teases, gripping my hip and pulling my dress back down. "You're so fucking sweet when you come."

"You're so good at that." I hide my face partially behind my hands.

"Anytime, babygirl. You just say the word. Trust me, it's no hardship tasting you." He pulls my hands away and kisses my cheek with a sensual chuckle that nearly curls my toes. "Are you feeling better?"

"Yeah, thank you. I think being around you and Sage is pushing my body a little, even with the suppressants." I don't say anything more than that, mostly because I can tell that Calder already knows what that implies. My first real heat would be arriving. If my intuition is right, and the tidbits of information I'm piecing together about Everette are correct, it's most likely going to hit sooner rather than later at the rate we're going, too.

"We'll take care of you, Opaline. I promise, you and your omega are safe with us. All of us."

All of us.

30

Calder

Rubbing my hands together, I reach for the purple and ivory colored bag with a big logo on it and pull out our dessert. Opening the container, though, I chuff. "Well..."

"What?" Snapping the flimsy lid back in place, I pull out the second container of Ethyl's and confirm it's also mutated into a liquid. Facing Opal, she's lying on her side watching me with her chin propped on a palm. "What is it?" She perks up trying to peek at the mess in my hands.

Tripping over my response a little, I finally get out, "A certain little omega distracted me, and it seems our ice cream melted," I tsk.

Her full laugh hits me like sunshine. "Moi!" A small hand demurely lands on her chest as she displays her clearly genuine outrage.

"Yes, you. Naughty thing."

"Mmhmm. I see. Well, do we need a moment of silence for Ethel's Ice Cream?" I damn near twist my neck to look at her, studying her face to confirm she's joking and messing with me.

"Honestly, maybe! I was pretty damn excited for you to try it," I huff, setting the containers back in the bag.

She wears a phony frown, fighting her own damn smile.

"Is my omega teasing her alpha?" I tilt my head, prowling closer, and growl playfully, sucking a rogue bit of creamed sugar from my thumb.

"No, never! I just want to support you in your grieving for your ice cream puddle properly." Her chin dips, eyes widening innocently in the way puppies do when they're caught, just before their reprimand.

Smirking, with a thoughtful hum, I continue, "I can think of another sweet puddle I'd like to be tongue deep in." Those kiss-swollen lips open in shock at my words, and I take the opportunity to pounce on my little prey, settling over her. "Would my sweet girl like that? Huh?" The tip of my nose traces abstract shapes along her neck, my lips stopping along the route, ending with a superficial bite. Not deep enough to penetrate or claim. But the response it elicits is exactly as I hoped, the effect immediate as she freezes and submits. "Mmm, there's my good girl. That's better." Getting the sweet little whimpers I wanted, I force myself to pull back, not missing her indignant expression at the distance I create between us. "You need to eat, babygirl." I turn and reach for my phone, confirming the chirp that sounded while I was enjoying my omega was in fact the food delivery confirmation. A quick peek at the photo tells me it was left on the patio by the door. Guess the extra thirty bucks was enough for the driver to bring it all the way to the building here and not drop it at the main lodge. "I'll go grab it and stop by the kitchen to reheat it if it needs it."

A little squeak follows as I shut the door behind me, lips tipped to the side.

This is my future, I'm sure of it.

The screen on my phone lights up and I reach for it, trying to avoid waking the woman half on my chest, snuggled up to me and a stuffed animal. Seeing Sage's name, I press on his text to open the thread, immediately regretting it.

Sage Fletcher

Soooo, uh. What's up?

What do you mean, what's up?

Good god, grandpa. How's the date with our omega?

Duh.

It's perfect. She's perfect.

What are you two doing right now?

She passed out after a series of events that tuckered her out.

A series of events? wtf does that even mean.

Like… a sexy series…?

That's between us.

WHO am I going to blab to!

Everette's in outer space and Adrian is Adrian

Plus I told you earlier…

Go to bed Sage.

K! Putting on shoes now, be there soon!

I meant your bed.

Are you in her bed together?

Are you snuggling?

Is she asleep?Aww is she snoring?

Yes, yes, and… a little

I'm coming over.

You're not.

Save me a corner. Tiny one.

I'll be silent.

You can't hog her.

I'm not hogging her. She fell asleep after our date.

1 – That's a lifelong joke waiting to happen, just so you know.

And 2 – I'm eating shitty chips and watching game show reruns from decades ago ALONE like a loser. Be nice.

lol

I won't even touch her. Just wanna look. Scout's honor.

I don't think it counts if you were never a scout.

I was. Got kicked out for being too cute. All the other kids jealous. So mean. Still sad.

Are you really coming…?

I'm already in my suv, responding at the stoplights. Said I was coming!

Unbelievable

Sure enough, shortly after our conversation, I knew he'd been telling the truth and was here. I could feel his presence on the opposite side of her door before the telling beeps, unlocking it.

Through a tiny crack as it slowly opens, I see his grinning face, attention snapping to the omega in my arms. I give him a pointed look and roll my eyes a little. Stepping inside, he toes off his shoes and draws a heart in the air with both pointer fingers. At that, I'm trying not to laugh and accidentally jostle Opal.

"Aw, you did save room for me. Big softy," he whispers. "I missed her." Standing on the side of the bed, Sage tugs his shirt off from behind his head and then reaches for his pants, undoing the zipper.

"Hey..."

"What..?" he pauses.

"I don't know that she'd be entirely comfortable with you naked, skin-to-skin with her yet. I'd rather have her awake and able to actively consent."

He considers and nods seriously. "You're right." He looks a little sad at the thought, like maybe he can't snuggle, running options in his head. His hand unconsciously rubs his stomach like a golden retriever desperate for calming belly rubs. "Should I wear my clothes in bed? You hate that." I knew he wouldn't be able to 'just look'. I don't blame him one bit.

"Shirt on, pants off, boxers on."

"Yes, Daddy Calder," he somewhat mocks with a face that annoys me.

"Stop calling me that, damn it." He seems to notice I'm still wearing my white undershirt too, glancing and noticing the pile of dark denim in the corner. Nodding, he drops his pants and ungracefully pulls his gray t-shirt back on hastily. Pulling the cover and sheet back, he slides in behind Opal, incredibly gently, with how obviously excited he is to be back this close to her.

Running his nose in her hair, he sniffs and smiles. "Smells so good."

"Certainly does." I hum, showing my agreement.

Watching Sage try to get fully comfortable in the small portion of the bed without falling off is comical enough that I can't stop my laugh, careful not to wake our omega. "Tight squeeze?"

"One, that's what she said. Two, this bed fucking sucks." It very clearly is not designed for a small pack to be crowded into. Who would have thought our staff lodging, typically for traveling singles, didn't have huge mattresses.

Sighing, I finally take pity on him, wrapping Opal in my arms and move her fully onto my chest, splayed on top of me, clearing room for Sage to push in, giving him more space. She adjusts slightly, unconsciously scent-marking me by rubbing her cheek against my chest and burrowing closer. There's no better feeling in the world than having my omega in my arms, safe and cared for.

"I gotta say, I'm impressed. I was expecting all the grace of a baby panda."

"Rude, brother. Plain rude." Sage settles, cuddled up to both Opaline and me. And, honestly, it feels good. It feels right having them so close. The brief thought of all of us together in her nest, Everette and Adrian with us, quickly proves me wrong, though. No, *that* would be the best feeling in the world. Our pack, finally complete.

His fingers toy with the ends of her hair, entirely dark in the dimly lit room. I trace freckles on her forearm and the silk of her new nightgown as we enjoy the beauty of the moment, the crickets sounding from the cracked window, the curtain flowing slightly and easily from the small breeze.

"This is the best night ever," he whispers reverently. Truthfully, as simple as it was, I couldn't agree more.

Our omega sighs, almost happily, in her sleep. Like, she too, agrees.

"Hey, Cald?"

"Yeah?"

"We're going to need to get her a bigger bed..."

31

Opaline

The general manager gives me a bit of a curious look, glancing down at the dress I have on. It's the same dress and jacket I wore last night on my date with Calder. I'm hoping she sees it as an overeager woman wanting to make a good first impression by dressing up. The truth of the matter is simply that I still do not have clothes clean enough that I would feel good about wearing.

However, the guys filled me in this morning before they left, and we chatted a bit about the position they had planned for me. We went a few rounds going back and forth with them offering something else, if I would want to do something else, or if I wanted to not work at all. But, honestly, what they had originally planned for the mystery homeless omega is exactly perfect. I can't think of anything better, still, after a couple of hours alone in my head.

"Okay, dear, if you want to follow me, we can get started?"

"Great!"

We're in the main lodging building, however, a bit hidden in some back hallways. I assume this area isn't available to guests, watching her pull a rectangular badge clipped to her well-formed suit jacket and pressing it towards security pads as we go. Noticing me following her movements, she adds, "Don't worry, I'll have your badge, uniforms, and name tag ready for you shortly. We weren't sure when you were planning to start, and the morning got away from me a bit. Otherwise, I would have had everything prepared prior." Her tone speaks of mild regret, like she really is sorry to not have things perfect for a new employee. Even a low-level one like me. The thought strikes me, and I hope this extends to other areas of her personality. It'd make a huge difference to have someone kind to work for. I also feel an immediate relief at the thought she has uniforms for me to wear.

Truthfully, I've been envisioning another nightmare like their events manager, Annabelle. But, considering everyone so far today, albeit the few I've met, have been very nice. I'm hoping Annabelle is a fluke on the larger scale. I should trust my alphas to have the sense to hire good people. "No problem at all, take your time," I respond, hoping I come off genuine as well. The smile I get in return says I do. It feels good, really good actually, to have so many nice interactions with people that aren't Sage or Calder. All of my new interactions with staff and even people from our visit into town are building what I hope may be a lovely preview into what my life could actually look like here as a whole. Not just known as the guys' omega. But, as me, as Opaline.

The majority of the opulence that comprises the lodging ends beyond these few halls. It still feels cozy and welcoming, in a simplistic kind of way. Walking along the maroon carpet, I follow Jewel. Her scent tells me she's a beta. Her steps are confident, and she's about the same height as me, which was nice. I tend to be taller than most women.

"Alright, and here we are. This will be your little work-home!" The cute phrasing catches me a little off guard. But she knows nothing about me and has zero reason to believe that the simple, ordinary word 'home' would be a bit of a trigger to my emotions. I hope one day it won't be anymore.

Walking inside the room, it's big, but not overly so. The flooring is a pretty green, square-tiled material. The walls, a neutral, soothing cream. A couple of large windows that nearly reach the floor with sheer curtains to match the floor make me smile. Being able to look outside, have a breeze, and enjoy the sounds of the resort as it runs naturally will be wonderful. I wonder if I could get peeks at Calder or Sage sometimes as they're passing this side of the building. That makes me smile even bigger, biting my bottom lip to hide it.

Glancing around for the full picture, it seems incredibly clean and well cared for, for what it was. There's a soapy, sterile fragrance lingering in the air. Not the smell of laundry soaps or softeners; I'd assume they use all scent-neutralizing products. It's the scent of sprays, glass cleaner, and most likely a mopping solution. It's pleasant.

Jewel takes a few steps around the space, offering a gestured hand at everything she points out to me and explains. "Alrighty. Well, I think most of this is self-explanatory. Washers. Dryers. Table for folding. Sorting bins, both for clean and dirty. Detergents and fabric softeners. And, this over here..." She takes a few steps and points towards a thin-looking pole with a massive clamp on the top that looks adjustable. "...is where you can clip the ends of sheets and blankets to help make folding easier. Little trick you might not know, and Lottie may forget to touch on it. But trust me, it will make your job much easier. Umm.. quick checklist on the clipboard that lives over here. Just make sure after your shift, you initial and complete each line item; pretty easy stuff, don't worry." She smiles and shrugs a little, stopping to check her phone as it chimes in her hand. "I think that's the gist. And, Lottie just let me know she's on her way over so she can walk you through everything more in depth. This used to be her last position before she asked to become a housekeeper. Tips are pretty generous for them. This position as Laundry Services Attendant seems to be an entryway into those positions as they open up. Doesn't happen often, though. Pack Morrison takes good care of their employees, so we tend to stick around." At their mention, I kind of blush a bit, but I'm not sure why. Feels oddly like pride.

"It's perfect. Thank you so much."

"No problem. Well, if you want to nosey around and hang out here, Lottie will be here in just a few minutes. Sound good?"

"Great! Thanks again."

"Nice to meet you, Opaline. First day's the hardest. You'll be great." I watch as the door slowly shuts behind her, silence overtaking the space, now alone in the laundry room. To suddenly have people supporting me was still hard to process and soak in. I've never had this before. Something so simple as Calder and Sage telling me I'd do wonderful, and this woman I don't even know, reassuring me the same, instead of snide remarks and sneers, gave me a feeling that I could really do things. It makes me even more excited to try and prove them right in having faith in me.

"Yoo-hoo! Hello!" A melodious, feminine voice sounds from the door, getting my attention. "Hi."

"Hi! Nice to meet you..."

"Opaline, right?"

I nod at her request for confirmation. "Anddd, Lottie?"

She laughs a little, grin huge and contagious. "You got it." Her free hand swings up between us, and I shake it in response. There's something about her energy that makes everything she does seem...charming. A mass of beautiful strawberry blonde hair that looks as though...like her tanned skin, has also been slightly affected by the sun. To say she's stunning nearly felt like an insult. She's breathtaking and captivating to just look at. With bright blue eyes practically sparkling, she goes on, "Sorry, it took me a bit longer to make my way here. Jewel's Assistant Manager stopped me on the way and pulled me into their office to scoop up your stuff. Hope that's okay!"

"More than, thank you."

"Yep, here ya go." She uses both hands to pass me the stack of folded forest green fabric, which I assume are the uniforms, and a couple of smaller items. Looking them over, I realize they're my magnetic name tag and a white badge on a lanyard. "Your uniform will look like these bad boys." She turns and stretches out the fabric of her shirt, spinning as if to show me. "They're pretty comfy. Like stretchy PJs. Could be worse."

I realize again I now have the space and opportunity to wash my other clothes, on top of the fact, I now have a stack of clothing I can wear daily for the next three days. Although I may have to try to do that after my shift. I can't help but hold the stack to my chest. I'm sure it doesn't feel like a big deal until you've lived out of a suitcase with no steady source of running water. It hit then, with what a huge blessing literally all of this has been, and how easily it could be ripped away. Only now, if I lost everything, I'm not sure I would really survive. Not losing Calder and Sage, my pack, my scent matches, my dream come true.

As if sensing my thoughts, Lottie points out my dress. "I love your dress, by the way! It's gorgeous." I don't know if she knows, but that comment puts me at ease immediately, like a shameful weight's been lifted. I wasn't weird, I wasn't broken, I shouldn't be embarrassed.

I am worthy.

32

Opaline

Charlotte —*er,* Lottie, can't stay long since she's still just starting her workday as well. She had this position last and is able to walk me through some basics and show me a binder she had put together on slower days a while ago, before leaving, though.

Honestly, everything she included in it is incredibly helpful. She goes over all the products, how to time things out on what days, and during the busiest times, so the rest of the team and spa staff never run out of towels. She mentioned once Tiffany bit her head off for not having the ability to make hot towels for her massages, and I want to really, really avoid that particular brand of conflict if possible. Any question I can think to ask, truthfully, is covered, even if briefly, in the documents she had printed and written on.

Luckily, today is a little slow. A large bulk of people checked out yesterday. So, today is the day any leftover linens and towels get washed, plus this morning's checkouts. A couple of bins sit sorted and filled next to the row of industrial washers, and a couple of empty ones next to the dryers.

Working to finish the small load of fluffy white towels, I stand on the squishy mat next to the oversized table, sorting. The movements and white noise of the machines running is nearly meditative. Reaching this corner to that, folding here, hot-dog style to hamburger style; it becomes repetitive in a really soothing way. Something I can do and focus my hands on while getting lost in thought here and there.

Time ticks by, pulling a humming song from my throat, my body and arms feeling a little looser and freer. I realize in the midst of meditative thought, that the feeling I'm experiencing is contentment. I'm happy and at...peace. For a moment, I just let myself feel it. I don't try to skip past it, convince myself otherwise, or even think of what the worst outcome could be to protect myself. I just sit with it, closing my eyes. It feels like so much that was buried a little too deep to be felt any other time is being pushed to the surface all at once, warmth and wetness starting to line my lashes. Taking a breath, I wiggle my shoulders a bit, blinking away the moisture, and slowly bring myself back into the room I'm standing in.

As if somehow my subconscious senses them, I turn on instinct to glance out the sunny window behind me. Sage's beautiful, tanned skin, black hair, and grin stare back at me behind the reflective glass. Gripping my chest a little and gasping in surprise, his fingers tap on the glass, Calder stepping in closer behind him, his own brown hair shifting slightly from the breeze. "Hey, Princess!" His words are a bit muffled, but have the effect I'm sure he was hoping for.

Stepping closer, I can't help but shake my head and smile, reaching to push up the large window. It brings us so close to being face to face Sage leans in and pouts a little that there's a screen in our way, preventing him from touching me. Gripping something small on each side, he starts to pull the screen down, Calder's voice follows, almost chastising without any real seriousness behind it. More humor and exhaustion. "Sage, come on, man."

All he does in response is shrug and set aside the screen he makes look like the weight of a piece of paper. Leaning back in a second time, he hums happily, warm hands gripping my cheeks and plump lips softly connecting with my own. My hands find his shoulders of their own accord, basking the attention and admiration my alpha's giving me. They haven't done anything other than make me feel special and wanted. I want to believe it so badly, but I fear there may always be that tiny part of me always prepared for the worst.

Calder pushes his packmate to the side, large hands already on my skin to steady me. "Hi, babygirl."

"Hi," I whisper back, softer and a little more shy than I mean to. His golden eyes bore into mine, the feeling of being the center of this man's attention overwhelming.

"My perfect, sweet omega." He follows Sage's example and leans in for a kiss. Closing, I let my vision fade and fall into the feel of his touch on my hip and the other hand behind my neck, melting.

"Hey!" Sage's outrage is evident, snapping my eyes open, back to the room. "I want another one. Mine didn't last that long." I bite the side of my lip to hold in my smile as Calder pulls back.

"Whose fault is that?" he smirks, eyes still wholly on me.

If I thought his outrage was obvious before, it's more than evident now. The sound he releases and Calder's expression make me wonder how frequently exchanges like this happen between the two of them. "UH, yours!"

A full, bright laugh escapes me, shaking my chest. I love watching them interact, more like brothers than packmates. "What are you guys up to?" I interrupt, putting a detour to their squabble.

"Few things on the books to check on here, but mostly just finance and backend stuff, marketing check-ins and whatnot that we do from home generally. We wanted to check on you. Before we could make it through the door like most humans, Sage saw you and couldn't stop himself from waiting another ten seconds." Calder winks, and Sage shrugs, both of them smiling. "How's the first day so far?"

"It's honestly...perfect. I'm loving it so far. And, everyone's been so kind today. Lottie and Jewel have been great." I want to be sure to mention them and how helpful they've been. Because they truly have. Chatting and laughing a bit with Lottie was genuinely fun this morning.

"I'm happy to hear it, baby." He tugs lightly on the ends of my hair, peeking over at the dark-haired beauty next to him. "What do you think of eating dinner with us tonight and telling us all about it?"

"I'd love that." The words couldn't ring more true. The longer I'm away from them, the more I'm already starting to miss them.

The guys speak at once, their words falling atop the other.

"You got it."

"Hell yes. More omega snuggles."

More omega snuggles indeed.

33

Sage

"We need to get her a phone," Calder's deep voice rings out as we walk.

"I know. I was thinking the same, actually. I keep going to text her, and don't have a way to be in contact. Not even an email address. I don't like it, and neither does my alpha." I want to constantly be texting or calling if I can't be hugging her all day.

Calder grunts, but I know he feels the same. "I understand she needs and wants a little space to be independent for a while. I respect that, and I'll do anything she wants. But, I do feel a little like I'm not doing my best as her alpha if I'm not constantly with her or checking in. You know?"

"Yep." I blow a breath from my lips that vibrates and comes out as a pathetic laugh towards the end.

"The other night when we left her food, I almost said fuck it and slept in the lounge in the staff lodging just to be near her." He laughs and shakes his head a little. "Insane." Little did he know I practically had to handcuff myself to my bedframe to stop myself from doing the same, only in the fetal position outside of her room with my ear to her door.

We approach the truck, Cald taking the driver's side, the telling beep of the doors being unlocked sounding. With grunts and groans that men in their thirties should probably not be making, we shut the doors and get situated. I'm in my own head enough that it takes me more than a few seconds to realize we're just sitting in a silent vehicle staring into nothing. Honestly, I don't really even care. Everything that doesn't include looking at or touching a pretty redhead kind of started losing its flair pretty damn quick.

"You think she really had a good first day?" I ask, knocking my boots together at the tips, arms crossed over my chest. "They better have been nice to her. You think she was hot in there? She didn't even have the windows open. Maybe we should get her a fan too. Oh, you know what?" I perk up. "Let's get some headphones too. She—"

"Jesus, Sage," Calder mutters, grinning. "You want to march back inside and inspect the laundry room for yourself? She was fine. More than fine, actually. She looked genuinely happy and contented."

Fuck, if it wasn't hot there, it's getting hot in here. I can already feel my hairline and ass sweating. I mutter a "Maybe." But that's just in response to his question about whether I want to go back and inspect it. Stupid question. Of course I do. I reach my arm over and press down the button to start the truck, annoyed when it won't start without his assistance. "Will you press your foot on the damn brake already? I'm burning up, how are you not?"

"You'll live. Imagine Ever going ten days without AC right now."

"He doesn't have air conditioning?" I practically gasp. "That's inhumane! There's no way. With the fancy-shmancy place he probably went to, there's no way." I can feel myself getting anxious and worked up, but I can't pinpoint why. Too many things.

"Sage, take a breath for me. It's not that hot, you're fine. And, we're going to go buy Opaline a phone right now and whatever else you want to throw in, okay? We'll see her for dinner tonight, too. Get this done, focus on work for a while, and then we get to see our omega. Good?"

I nod, silently, watching as he starts the truck and reach to adjust my vents.

"Good. Now, take a few deep breaths." I do as he says, because of course he's right. I'm kind of freaking out over nothing. But only a little. "Good." He reaches over and squeezes my shoulder, grounding me a bit. I appreciate him so much. I don't think I could even imagine a life where he wasn't in it.

We drive for a while without saying anything else. The trees are all a lively green, flowers in bloom, adding spots of color everywhere. I like just looking at things. I know it sounds weird. But, I do. Going for scenic drives, watching a sunset, watching people, surroundings. Didn't exactly match me as a whole. Calder compares me to a puppy sometimes. If he didn't have so many treats, I wouldn't give him a free pass.

His low voice catches my attention. "I'm really proud of her. You know?" I absolutely do know. She's the strongest person I've ever met. I've spent the last several nights thinking the same, among an unending list of others, all about her. "Everything she's been through, and she's already doing so well, and then even going so far as to starting her job already. She deserves the world."

I can't help but really and truly smile at that. Because unsurprisingly, we again are on the same page. "Yeah, she does." My bottom lip fills the space between my teeth, smile still stretching my face. A triage of images start flying through my mind of what our future could look like...all of us.

"Seriously? How many phone cases do you think she's going to go through, exactly?" Calder raises a brow towards me from the center island in the store. We're surrounded by cellphones, speakers, tablets, and a million-and-one accessories. The young 'kid' on the other side of the table to Cald somehow looks bored and terrified of the giant in front of him. I can't help but fully laugh at the image. I'm used to him, but, every now and then, I'm reminded of how others must perceive his size.

"I'm not getting her all these because I think she's going to be, like, throwing her phone off the roof every day or something. I don't know, maybe she wants to coordinate with her clothes, ya know? Or maybe one day glitter feels right and pink doesn't? Better than whatever boring, not cute, B.S. you'd pick out." I mutter the last part, mostly because he kind of already looks like he's at capacity for my shit today, and I still have the rest of the afternoon and evening with him. Maybe he hears me, because he stalks over and starts looking over the wall of cases. "Oh, look at this one! It's got little floating purple and gold stars like a snow globe! Damn, how cute is that?"

Glancing over, Cald acts like it isn't the best one. Probably because I found it first. "Looks like it was pushed out of a unicorn's ass."

"I know... It's perfect."

He shakes his head, fingers touching and moving over several cases hanging in front of him. "Whatever. Fine. But that's the last one. Don't over do it."

"Uhh, sir?" Called over by the employee, he steps away. A wide smile stretches my lips as I see a pop-socket assortment. Those would be perfect for her to maybe prop up her phone and watch shows while she's folding laundry, all adorable-like. Actually...wait.

"Should we get her a tablet, too?" I raise my voice towards Calder.

"I was thinking that. But, I don't want to overwhelm her with too much at once." I definitely don't miss the pointed look at the small mesh basket I have filled.

"We could get it and just give it to her later? We're already here," I shrug, throwing in a couple of the little round things before walking over and dumping the basket on the countertop.

Calder hums, but ultimately agrees. I'm going to assume, with the way the kid's eyes get a little wider, finally noting all the shit we plan on buying, that he gets some sort of commission or credit for the sales numbers.

"I can't wait to text her. I'll feel better knowing she can be in touch with us immediately, whenever she wants. If she needs anything, whatever. Ya know? Two in the morning, I'll find a way to get it for her."

Cald chuffs, rubbing his hand down his face with a smile, albeit a bit warily. "That offer extend to packmates?"

"Do you have long, pretty hair, a pussy, and smell like sugared heaven?" The younger employee sputters a bit, obviously having heard me. Calder bites his cheek to stop from smiling. I'm certain of it. Any moments I can gather of Calder loosening the reins on the serious pack lead vibe feel like a win.

We're all pretty damn close to the same age, somehow. I've met packs that have fairly severe age gaps, but it seems to all work out. I feel like sometimes Calder puts too much on himself as our lead. Forced to be the 'older', wiser one of us.

I wish he wouldn't.

My mind conjures up images of Adrian, and I know confidently that it's eating Calder alive. I keep wanting to bring it up, even wondering if it's ultimately my business. But, it abso-fucking-lutely is. His actions, even if mild right now, will affect and potentially hurt the now center of my entire universe. It hasn't been long, so I feel like maybe he just needs more time. But eventually, this has to be handled head-on. And if Calder won't. I will.

Opaline hasn't brought it up in the last few days since arriving, yet either, but I know it's there. Of course it is. We don't keep secrets as a pack, and Calder told me about her being able to open up and be vulnerable with him after their date. This is her dream too. Not just mine or ours. But hers, too. I see the questions in her eyes, the hesitancy to ask. With the little that she knows, I kind of understand why. I'm not sure we painted him in the best light, looking back now. She's working with breadcrumbs. I internally curse, replaying what little we've shared.

Adrian is not a bad person. The furthest thing from it, actually. He's devoted, loving, kind, and insanely loyal. But *relationships,* particularly omegas, are the single thing that will push him over the edge, or shut him down completely. I haven't even seen him since shortly after working together on the grounds plumbing issue. That means he's constantly working, hiding in the greenhouse, or doing shady shit on his Harley, sneaking in and out of the house when we're not there or while we're passed out.

I'll give it a couple of weeks. I think that's more than fair. If it's not addressed by then, I'll bring it up. Everette will be back by then, and the three of us can sit down and handle this together.

There. I take a deep breath, and immediately I feel better knowing I have a timeline and a plan.

Now, time to buckle in and get shit done so I can get back to my princess.

34

Opaline

It's such a beautiful night.

The sun's already set as we walk under the twilight-tinted sky. Crickets and other sounds that remind me of long-ago summers spent outside echo like white noise everywhere around us. Closing my eyes, I take a deep breath and simply feel into the warmth on my skin, the sounds, and the small breeze. It's all so perfect.

The sounds of gravel crunching underfoot catch my attention, and Mom's smiling at me, her dark hair beautiful and shining under the freshly awakened moonlight. "You have no idea how proud of you I am, my little Opal gem." I can't help but chuckle, the smile on my own face stretching to its limits. She used to always call me that.

Vaguely... something about that thought stands out as odd, though.

"What could you have to be so proud of?" I ask, joking but a little serious. Walking together, we move forward, the beautiful, dark lake to our right. Lush, full, green trees line both sides of the gravel road we're on. Little solar lights help guide the way. Her voice echoes in my head, and with sudden clarity, I freeze, looking to her only to see her sad, loving smile back at me. "You...you're not really talking. Your lips

aren't moving..." Like a wave, the emotion and memory of her death hit me so hard, I can't breathe.

Her hand reaches out to cup my face.. but I don't feel it. I don't feel it?

"You... you left me," I whimper, tears now falling freely.

"My sweet girl. I may have left you on this earth for now. But, it's not goodbye." Her smile carries a light to it I haven't seen in so long.

"What do you mean?" I shake my head, face crumpling and lips trembling.

"This life is just a small experience, just a stop compared to what's waiting."

"I don't understand? What's waiting?"

"More love than you could possibly comprehend right now." She traces her eyes over my face, and I realize that's the light in her I hadn't felt in so long...love. "We're all here, at home, waiting. This is your chance to be human for a while. Go, have fun, feel every emotion, connect with the spirits of nature, simply be and simply exist in this form...truly live and lean into your intuition. It'll bring you exactly what you need. We all love you more than you could possibly know. We're here watching and rooting for you, always. Look for the signs... I'm always with you."

Sobs shatter free, wracking my body. Squeezing my eyes shut, I try to feel her hand just one more time as she reaches for my cheek again. But there's nothing... Opening my eyes, there's nothing...

"No... No. Mom! Wait.." I gasp, trying to suck in air, looking around like she could be hiding. But, she's not here...

I jolt awake, gasping for air. Adrenaline pushes my body out of bed, the urge to run and move overwhelming me. The sheet and blanket tangle around my legs, holding my calves as the rest of me tumbles off the bed, onto the cold floor.

Those few seconds are all I need to start to come back to reality, realizing I was running from a dream. It wasn't real... I'm here in my room at the resort. Alone.

The tears are real, though. The darkness feels pressurized and suffocating in the small, confined space, somehow made worse by the wet tracks drying on my cheeks. Twisting, I fight the covers until my legs are free, registering parts of me are covered in a sheen of sweat, as are parts of the bedding. I still mildly feel like I'm floating, my balance uneven as I rush to stand. Desperate for comfort, I fumble and search for the single constant I've had for years. "Sparkles... Sparkles..." I murmur her name, shoving pillows and bedding back until I find her buried. Pulling her to my chest, the weight in her tummy's what I need to start to feel even remotely grounded and connected to reality again.

I loved the rare times I would dream about my mother. But even when the dreams are good, it still feels like all the energy is pulled from my body, leaving behind a mess of emotion and lingering, unresolved grief.

Forcing myself to take slow, deep, even breaths, I keep Sparkles to my chest and search for the guys' clothes they had left here. Pulling on Sage's sweats and Calder's shirt, it's enough to nearly send me into a fresh, different spiral; their scents so comforting it actually somehow hurts.

It feels like my emotions are right under the surface, the chaos of everything left unfelt and unhealed for years pushing upwards at once. Vaguely, I wonder if this is because my heat will be starting soon. The change in hormones can't be helping anything at the very least.

The feeling of out swimming a giant sea monster as it chases me through dark, deep waters rings true and I'm seconds away from being swallowed. I can't handle it. I need to get away.

When the urge to flee and find fresh air and open sky presents itself, I do nothing to deny it. I need a bit of familiarity. Sadly, what had become my norm, sleeping under the stars is what I know to be familiar.

Without doubting myself, that's exactly what I do.

35

Opaline

The blast of cool night air greets me as I slip through the side door of the building. The breeze on the air wraps around me, twisting my hair this way and that, but I can finally breathe. In no longer than a moment, the air seems to still and settle, the whirlwind around me coming to a close as the quiet of the night and its surroundings become clear. It feels like even the wind spirits know I need their gentle support right now. I only remember bits and pieces of our conversation in my dream. But, leaning into the spirits of nature is foggily lingering as advice she'd left me with.

This is exactly what I need. Closing the door behind me silently, I turn, Sparkles still to my chest. Her weight is a very real comfort I can't explain to anyone. Objectively, I know I look and sound insane, being this attached to a stuffed animal that does not, in fact, have a conscience. But when you're lonely and isolated with not a single person to lean on, it doesn't seem quite so crazy.

Over time, night after night, no one but her to talk to, to vent to, other than the night sky, she became more important to me than most people were. Now, I know the day will come when our relationship will fade if my future keeps moving towards and evolving with my alphas. Which I desperately want, more than life itself, to be honest. But that's something for another day.

Gaze exploring the sleeping greenery and various buildings, the resort lands seem bright in comparison to the darkness of my bedroom. Unending stars blink and shimmer in the expanse of sky. Every direction, as far as I can see, is unpolluted by lights and glowing with stars. Somehow, it's both soothing and leaves a bit of sadness to sit with.

Without preamble, my feet are urged forward. The path below me is softly lit with the same small solar lights that illuminate all the resort walkways, just enough to make out the way ahead. I don't second-guess myself or my intuition for leading me in any certain way. I just trust and keep one foot in front of the other.

As I walk, the night is quiet. Critters and crawlies are a little quieter too, offering respect to their mother nature as she rests. Hidden in the tree line, an owl's hoot echoes through the shuffle of flowing leaves in the depth of trees. Instead of scaring me, wandering the darkness alone, the sounds are reminders of where I am, setting me at ease. I genuinely wonder if these grounds are blessed by the gods or ancient energies beyond our understanding with the beautiful, distinct energy felt here. Or maybe it feels magical to me in the few days since I'd arrived, simply because to me, it's a real-life haven.

The further I go, the darker it gets, and any lights that do happen to be on from the main resort mostly fade. Without noticing, I've left the stone path, reaching the end of their property, or at least the end of the resort itself. It's nearly open space ahead. A wide field, pushing the trees further back.

My feet come to a stop, holding my body in place in the tall, tickling grasses as they move under the weight of the breeze. Dandelions are plentiful, poking their heads out every couple of feet. I stand and simply look around, taking in the image before me, arms wrapped around me with Sparkles close. A soft wind hits my cheeks, blowing strands of my hair behind me. I find myself briefly closing my eyes and smiling, genuinely enjoying these quiet minutes, finding my center again.

I love the stars, the night sky. It's what I feel connects me to my mother, even now, after all of these years. It's a rarity, but when I can, I talk to them, just like she taught me to. Only now, I speak as if I'm talking to her. The night sky has held me while watching me wipe away my tears too many times to keep count.

Just as shooting stars are supposedly rare, I have seen so many throughout all these years I've lost count of those moments, too. The part of me that dreams, wants to believe it's my mother letting me know she's still with me. Maybe these are signs she's trying to convey to me, from her. I don't know if I really believe it fully. But when things are just too much, it's one of the few things that can keep me going in what feels like a hopeless life. I suspect those days may come fewer and further in between though, given my recent blessings.

Taking a deep breath, I let it rush out, looking up at the sky. "Hi, momma...." I whisper the words, pulling pieces of grass to twiddle between my fingers. "I had another dream about you. So, I came out here to get some fresh air." I feel crazy saying these things out loud. But I figure I'm far enough away that no one can hear me. "It's crazy, even after all these years, I still miss you this much. Sometimes it feels like no time at all has passed. Like I'm still that younger version of me when you died."

Fuck, my heat is definitely coming soon. My emotions are overwhelming. It's too much when I feel things this deeply. Sighing, I continue. "Anyway, you always said the stars were for wishes. I spent all these years wishing for the same four things, over and over: true love, a safe place that felt like home, real friendships, and to have you back." I can feel my tears falling freely as the memory of her hangs around me, gripping my throat. "Now, I have a real chance at the first two...and it still hurts. Ya know?" I wipe away the tears clouding my vision and release a huff of air thickly through my lips. "Anyway, I love you just as much today as I did the last day you were with me down here. I miss you. I hope you can somehow hear me. I don't remember if I got to say in my dream, if that was...somehow really you. I love you."

Like a gift directly from her own hands, a tiny shooting star off in the distance streaks through the sky before disappearing into the dark. The sobs and tears shake my body, breaking free and blending with laughter. The sign is all too clear. I have to believe. I have to believe it's her. My heart feels like it's being cracked open. I collapse into the damp grass, Sparkles buried to my neck, and let myself release what I need to, dew clinging to my clothes and skin.

Sometimes, I feel so foolish and so embarrassed for holding so much hurt and pain from losing her. Holding on for so many years. But, I also wonder if maybe the severity of heartbreak from grief is a lesson we all have to find the beauty in. Grief only exists where love once lived. I think that's the saying, anyway.

I'm not sure how long I lay here, looking up. But eventually, I feel freer and lighter. The sense of gratitude starts filling the heavy space of sadness. Smiling softly, I stand, and with one last look, turn to go back to the staff lodging.

Only, I notice a golden light, I haven't seen before. Maybe coming from a building that looks unfamiliar.

Following the growing soft light, the image of what it truly is starts to piece together, and a gasp leaves my lips. The structure rises before me like a secret cave tucked halfway into the earth. There, half-built into a small hill and covered in what looks like frosted glass panes, is a beautiful greenhouse.

There is no doubt in my mind that's what this is. The soft glow from inside leaves shadows of various flowers against the sides, silhouettes like something out of a cottage in a fairytale. I can't believe the guys haven't shown me this! I can't help the immediate thought and wonder if they need help here instead of with the laundry.

Drawn forward, I pick up the pace and find the door, a huge smile stretching my lips.

Reaching forward, it opens with little effort with a soft creak.

36

Adrian

Spilled soil and cut leaves pile into the oversized dustpan as I sweep the broom weaving a pattern that's repetitive and nearly meditative. It's a quiet night after another long day of hiding. I feel the building fatigue deeply, weighing down my movements, in more ways than one. All I'm doing is buying myself time at this point while I finalize my plans. I'd spent the last couple of days putting together a resume and applying to jobs much like the one that brought me here.

I just never really imagined years later, I'd be back to square one, running again.

Only this time, it's so much worse. I have my pack family, finally. We're perfect together. They understand me and give me grace in the moments I need it. And I do everything I can to be what they need individually as their packmate, too. Everything I have in my life is because Calder took a chance on me all those years ago.

And it's all crashing down, again. All because of another omega...again.

I'm already so fucking tired.

Numbness from overwhelm hangs just outside of my skin, like a condensed layer of fog. Every time I feel overwhelmed or have too much thrown at me, it all converges into a numb nothingness. Honestly, that I can deal with more than the tsunami of emotion choking me and beating me down. I'd rather feel nothing than everything, too deeply.

There's the tiny, one percent of me that's sinking its wondering claws deeper and deeper, though. What it might be like, who she is, what she looks like. Could she really be my scent match, too? Statistically, it *is* highly likely. I know, simply because the only omega I'd ever accepted into my life was not my scent match.

It's the very reason she tragically died, and my world crumbled. The reason I begged for death for months, practically daring the universe to pull the trigger with the way I rode my fucking bike. Looking back, I can't believe I didn't die that first year after her passing, all the stupid, reckless shit I did.

My phone brightly lights up in the dim space, enlarging the nearby floral shadows and illuminating their petals and leaves. Setting the broom to the side, I walk over to check the name, anxiety flooding any sense of numbness that had claimed me. I fully expect it to be one of the guys. I've been waiting for them to lose their shit on me, tell me what a pathetic piece of shit I am, how I'm fucking up their lives and hurting their omega. I know it's coming. It's just a matter of time. And, if I can be gone before then, that would be ideal.

I'm a fucking coward, planning on leaving without saying anything. I know it's wrong, know it's literally the worst fucking thing I can do. The very thought honestly breaks me a little, making my chest tight, like an anvil is suddenly sitting on it. The idea to leave the family I'd built, that I'd dreamt of is sickening.

Breaking away from a pack just...isn't done. *Unless you're a worthless piece of shit.* The little voice in my head wastes no time in reminding me.

Alphas know who's pack, just like an omega and an alpha know they are scent-matches. It's partially scent, yes. But it's mostly an internal knowing from our inner alphas and the primal part of our brains. We just know. And I know Calder, Sage, and Everette are my pack with one hundred percent certainty.

I won't just be walking away from my potential scent match, my soulmate. I will be walking away from my pack brothers. Forever. Because this? This won't be forgivable. A foolish, terrified part of me knows that and wants to do it anyway because I'm so fucking terrified of losing another omega. And Natalie wasn't even my biological soulmate. Just the words feel wrong to think, nausea heavy in my stomach. I had loved her more than life. That was years ago.

Logically, and from what I know and have learned of scent matches, Natalie and I's relationship won't even compare to that of bond with their new omega. That terrifies me even more.

I'd spent hours at the main bar in town the last two nights, looking for a distraction and a way to drown my sorrows, even for a little while. Looking at my phone, it isn't Calder or even Sage. Certainly isn't my Everette. It's a woman I stupidly gave my number to while piss-drunk my first night out. I don't even have an interest in fucking her, to be honest. I don't want any connection, physical or otherwise, with anyone, even the eager-to-please pretty beta. She tried to tempt me for a bathroom blowjob. Just the offer turned me all the way off. More power to her if that's what she genuinely wants. It's just not what I want right now. With my current mood, I kind of want to tell her to fuck off and stop texting me incessantly.

Sighing, I toss the phone back onto the table and collapse into the couch next to it. The back quarter or so of the greenhouse is almost like an office or efficiency studio. It's even tucked underground. Before the guys bought the resort, this used to be the groundskeeper's room, from what I understand. Little odd. But, more than not, I get it. I've never had a single plant make me feel like I was going to throw up from the internal emotional noise they triggered.

I don't think the guys even realize I'm not sleeping at the house. I'm sure they're spending every second they aren't working with their omega. I have no idea if she's been up to the house yet. I'm too chicken shit to go back myself, instead crashing here in the greenhouse. That's part of the reason I told them it's off limits. I don't want her here. I don't need that added complication when I'm being crushed under the weight of everything else.

I will say, though, from the very few sentences Calder shared with me about her, it sounds like she's a fighter. They went to the city to help an omega that was homeless and alone, fucking sleeping behind his pop's bar. That alone is fucking insane and unacceptable. I might not interact with omegas anymore, but, their designation biologically tends to be more susceptible to illness, naturally smaller and more delicate than both betas and alphas, and unfortunately, is targeted for pretty unsavory shit.

The very fact that this woman, this omega, had survived on the street speaks volumes about who she is just as a person, as her. I respect that. It's one hundred percent the omega that my brothers deserve. We've all had people express interest in us, in us as a pack, for the entirely wrong reasons. We've even had families offering to make deals with us for arranged marriages. It's all because they see the resort and see our combined net worth, dollar signs flashing and cash raining down in their minds. Unfortunately, that's another aspect of omega and alpha relationships that I wish I weren't knowledgeable about.

My neck strains under the constant tension as I stretch and reach back to pull my shirt off, kicking my shoes off and lying out on the couch, feet hanging off the end. Reaching over, I pull the chain on the old-school lamp nearby, everything plunging into darkness. The lone wall separating this space from the greenhouse is translucent, like the rest of it. The area on the other side glows a little with a few solar lamps we had installed, as well as reflects natural lighting from the bright stars off the tables and shelves. Eyes closed, it isn't too bad, though.

Taking a few deep breaths, I try to slow my mind enough to fall into sleep, bombarded with a newly perpetual heartache.

37

Opaline

Tiptoeing lightly into the darkened, dimly space, it smells of soil and plants, confirming my greenhouse theory. The air is lush and floral under the heavy layers of earthly scents. The heat hits just as instantaneously, a humid warmth that chases away any lingering chill on my skin after standing outside and laying in damp grasses for a little too long.

Assessing my surroundings, I turn the doorknob behind me, closing what appears to be the only entrance or exit. Above, a huge dome meets in the center of the long space. What look to be baby trees sit directly below it's peak. I can't tell, and don't know enough about plants to know if they're actually baby trees, or not. Two rows of them back-to-back line the center of the greenhouse, hiding quite a bit from view at my current vantage.

With little exploration, I see there's an area to the right that's primarily shelving, stacked and loaded with all different kinds of plants. Colorful flowers and new buds stand out, even in the dark space as they sleep. It reminds me of the indoor hot springs they have, which I had fallen in love with immediately upon stepping inside during my tour. It feels the same in here, minus the tinkling sulfuric water. This must be where a majority of those plants and tropical trees come from.

Around the perimeter are various species of plants. I can't help but gently trace my fingers along the leaves and petals, some of which feel like velvet to touch. The further I wander, the more condensed and heavy the air seems to feel. Without much thought on it, I continue to stroll deeper, trying to place and recognize anything I might be familiar with. Sadly, neither in school nor at the Omega Care Facility did we have the opportunity to learn much about botany. We had touched on basic gardening at the OCF. But the knowledge obtained apparently was surface-level, as I try to test myself as I walk. Some frankly look otherworldly with their patterns and vibrant displays.

Every inch of this space is filled with beauty, housing the literal hum of life of each growing thing. Every few feet or so, more little lights are strategically placed. They assumedly don't appear to be grow lights; I imagine those would be much brighter, but they also don't seem like the dim solar lights that decorate the property either. They add the perfect amount of light to admire everything in the greenhouse. Stopping to bend and smell several flowers, I end with a small bunch of beautiful yellow and red spotted lilies. They've always been one of my favorites. With a small whisper of appreciation, I lean closer for a second sniff.

The greedy part of me wants to ask if maybe Calder would let me have one of the lily plants for my own room. I have no idea how to care for it, though. The image of Sage snatching one in secret conjures in my mind's eye, blooming petals peeking and bouncing behind his back as he offers it to me brings an audible giggle to slip from my lips.

With an inspiring awe, I make my way to the end of the overflowing rows and shelves.

38

Adrian

Even drifting in the space between realms, bordering on falling asleep, unease eats at me. A fog seems to force my weight into the cushions at my back, growing heavier and heavier, my limbs paralyzed. As terror lights my nerves, and I'm fighting to conjure all of my strength enough to pull myself out of whatever twisted dimension of hell this is, a glowing warmth appears. Closer and closer, the fog clears, the weight lifting completely, now nearly leaving me floating in comparison. A laugh sounds somewhere in the distance, pulling my lips up at the joy.

Another true, soft giggle loud enough to catch my attention calls me back to awareness, eyes blinking and consciousness coming back online as the joy fades. In the still of the night, always on alert, I catch it, albeit barely there, and realize the sound had infiltrated my dream-like state. I wait a few seconds for another indication of who's here, staying perfectly still, but none comes. It's silent. Closing my eyes, I focus my honed hearing on the other side of the frosted wall, wondering if I am actually asleep and dreaming it.

With all of my senses focused on one task, I'm able to hear the whispers of touch on the air. I've caught teenagers in here before trying to find a spot to fool around or just generally being little assholes. I ended up putting locks on the door to the private space here, but it seemed a little ridiculous to put them on our greenhouse door. They hadn't been trying to hurt anything. Just being nosey or brain-dead from all their blood rushing south.

Mustering all the stealth I'm capable of, I slowly stand and make my way to the door, fully prepared to scare the ever-loving-piss out of a young couple. Next to the door, I can hear the slightest murmurs and whispers, words unclear.

Saying fuck it, I silently twist the knob on my end of the door and pull it open a few inches and take a curious sniff, trying to catch a scent on the air.

In a violent rush, my alpha shoves past any restraints, jolting to the surface, putting the full force of my buried primal urges into action as I fight miserably to keep control. A vicious snarl leaves my throat in a deafening roar shaking the walls as the all-knowing sense of *mate* fills and expands every cell in my fucking body.

Both hands lock onto the door frame, my fingers cramping and throbbing from the force, stopping myself from doing anything insane. A piercing scream tears through the air, her distress and terror only calling to my alpha more. The primal and instinctual urge to fix and protect *mate. Omega.* My omega.

Her.

It's her, in front of me.

I vaguely realize a low snarling growl is still vibrating through me, tracing every move this woman makes, now visible before me. I lose the battle to hold my grip on the doorframe, falling forward slightly, fighting with everything I have to stay in control over my alpha.

Fisting my hands, I shake my head and close my eyes in an effort to ground myself, the nonstop snarl finally dying in my throat.

It doesn't stop me from striding forward, stalking what I know is mine, head tilting animalistically. Chest rising and falling, eyes wide, she trips over her own foot trying to back away from me, falling on her ass, yelping. The sound only reignites the vibration in my throat.

Fuck! I don't have control right now. One wrong move on either of our parts, and I don't know how the next few minutes might go. But there's no single part of me that can keep away from the call of her omega, terrified or not.

Every slight movement on her part simultaneously awakens the part of my alpha that wants to hunt. Wants her to run so I can chase and catch and claim with teeth buried in her neck as she comes around my cock, fucking her in the dirt as the forest's trees watch me prove who she belongs to.

"I'm s-sorry. I d-didn't m-m—"

"Omega..." The tenor of the word resembles the guttural rumble of a demon in the seventh layer of hell, only contributing to the tears falling down her flushed cheeks. Any rational thoughts are foggy, but I know I have to get my alpha locked up and under control.

Calder and I are equally driven by our alphas. Only, he's better equipped to handle his and obtain dominance when it pushes to the surface. I fought mine and buried it for so long, refusing its urges, that I now have less control than I fucking should. Virtually none. A point that's being made all too clear exactly now. Every part of me wants to care for this omega, to make sure she's fed, fucked, and tucked away in a nest filled with my baby.

I feel like I'm going insane, caught in a fog, in a different dimension. The prayer that this may all just be a nightmare courses deeply in the recesses of my mind.

I clench my jaw hard enough to crack my back teeth, fists tense at my sides. Forcing slow even breaths, I focus every ounce of energy I have in me to push my alpha down and handle this like I fucking need to, to put an end to this like I planned.

39

Opaline

My tremors chatter my teeth, every part of me buzzing with electricity and terror at the alpha in front of me.

I don't understand. My omega is just as confused as I am, too, which isn't a good sign. I know, and she knows, this is our mate. Our scent match. His fresh rain, cedarwood, and floral scent wraps around us with a level of intensity that I have never felt before. Not even when I met Calder and Sage. Every inch of my skin is layered in braille as more and more goosebumps spread quick as wildfire at his echoing snarls.

There is nothing gentle or loving about this man. Nothing that would make me guess this is Everette as the guys described him.

This has to be Adrian.

From his eyes, tense muscles, and the unending demonic and feral growl reverberating from his chest and throat, he screams *threat.* Even to me, his own omega. He has to smell me, to know I'm meant to be his.

"This area is off limits." His words are clipped and incredibly forced. Like, just getting them out is a huge feat. I feel like this moment is slipping away from me, and all my inner omega pleads to do is fix it. "Get. Out"

"Adrian?" I ask, trying to even my breathing. I know he's mine, and his alpha would never let him hurt me, even if he wanted to. Right? The thought is unspeakable.

"LEAVE!" He snarls, eyes piercing in their hate, doing nothing to ease the swelling level of panic holding me to the ground. The look in his eyes and instinct makes it clear running would be a disaster. I have to get to the door without provoking him.

I can't help it, I can't fight it. The whine that breaks free is something between an apology, frustration, terror, and confusion. "I'm sorry," I whisper, struggling to stand and step back with the tremor coursing through my body. He's tracking me and every inch that now separates us, chest still heaving. "I'm..." I start, but fight to get the words out. I don't even know exactly what I'm trying to say out loud. I just know the innate feeling that I'm drowning in, I need to get out between us. "Scent m-match." I stumble over the simple two words, but I see the moment they land. See the lift of his lips exposing his gums.

"That means *nothing*. You will never be my mate." Malicious intent and disgust coats his every word as he spews vitriol.

I stagger back at the impact of his words, like I'm feeling a part of my own heart stop beating. Any breath in my lungs is pushed out by the weight of despair now growing heavier by the second on my chest. Gasping to breathe is strength I don't have. *'You will never be my mate.'* His words tumble in my mind, leaving heartbreak in their wake.

"You don't... You don't mean that..." I whimper, not caring if I embarrass myself.

Instead of a response, all he does is turn back inside the place he appeared from and slam the door, the most vicious snarl I've ever heard shaking the frosted walls around me.

I can't stop running.

Not until the safety of my room surrounds me and I can call Calder and Sage. It's selfish and illogical, but I don't even care what time of night it is. I need them close to me. Any logical thoughts are lost and buried under adrenaline and residual terror.

My heart pounds out of my chest so terribly, it echoes the sentiment of something chasing me, but I don't look back. It isn't just pounding from running at a sprint. It's because of him, because of Adrian. His entire presence had hit and rolled over me, mirroring the likings of his scent, like a bad thunderstorm and tornado, leaving me trembling.

Adrian....

Even thinking his name makes my chest tighter, more tears springing to life as my feet pound. His scent somehow still lingers, and I wonder if I'm pulling it from imagination or if it was so potent in the tiny space it clung to my clothes and skin. Cedarwood, heavy rain on a spring day, and blooming flowers. That's what his scent feels like. A wild thunderstorm in the spring.

My omega had recognized him, and it wasn't subtle. There is no doubt he's mine. She had screamed, clawing to the surface at his presence, overwhelmingly so. I know it's because both my omega and I were waiting for what might now never come: our recognition bond snapping into place.

Meeting him was nothing like meeting Calder or Sage. There was no click of our bond, no rush of euphoria, comfort, or the feeling of home. Calder had scared me when he first saw and scented me. But, even then, reflecting, I knew he was safe. I was never *truly* scared.

There was none of that with Adrian. He doesn't even know me, and he hates me.

Hadn't he felt it, too? I know he had to have scented me. We're scent matches, I'm positive. Fuck, I don't know what to believe. Even if we are, why hadn't the bond snapped into place immediately? Had he really recognized me as his mate and...somehow rejected it in the moment? Is that even possible?

Maybe our bond isn't the part that's broken.

Maybe he is.

Maybe I am.

40

Sage

Yeah, so I did a creepy thing. Only a little creepy though.

This couch isn't as comfortable as I thought I remembered it being. I've also never tried to sleep on it, though. But it's warm at least, and wide enough for me to not fall off.

My ears strain to listen for anything from her room down the hall, but, there's nothing. I'm glad she's sleeping. She needs all the rest she can get, especially if her heat is going to be making an appearance soon. I guess a part of me was just hoping she'd text me in the middle of the night, excited about her phone, and ask me to come snuggle. Then I'd be all *'ta-dah!'* I'm already here...on the couch in the staff lodging community room. Perfect.

Hey, I own the damn thing. I can sleep on it if I want. In my full defense, it's not like I'm trying to form any habit of it long-term. I'm certainly not aiming to be *that guy*. 'Couch guy' as the staffers might call me. That'd be crazy. No, the goal is for her to move in with us, not me in here.

We had a great night tonight. Opaline, Cald, and I got dinner in town and then got ice cream. She kept giggling about ice cream soup to Calder. No clue what it means, but it made her light up from the inside. I think she's liking it here, which is a huge relief, but, she seemed to want some space tonight after we came to drop her off. Which is totally fine. Believe it or not, I do understand. She needs time to adjust and time to be alone, knowing she's safe and cared for. And today was another big day for her. She's had a lot of those.

So, we went home.

And then I left that home.

And came here. Still giving her space, but close enough to ease the stress my alpha is feeling, not being glued to her. I snicker, stopping myself from snorting out loud. Sure. 'Space', my ass, huh? So what if I'm a little obsessed with her? She's my fucking omega. Mine forever. That thought has me smiling cheesy, eyes closed in the dark room.

It's quiet, the low hum of the ceiling fan circulating above really the only sound outside of a faint murmur of nature and bugs outside. The windows are closed, though, so even that's extra faint.

I lay here for a while, listening for any sounds from her room, thoughts circling and bumping into each other in my brain. I start listening so hard, I hear my own heart and frown. There's a sudden restlessness dancing around inside me, my muscles lighting up with tension. I have no idea why. But, I don't like it. I physically have to stop myself from going to her damn room just to check on her.

I don't know how long passes, honestly. When I hear the tiny beeps from the door pad sounding, I'm on alert, tensing, though. I stay perfectly still in my spot on the couch, hidden. Employees are free to come and go as they please, obviously. But, this late?

Feather-light footsteps inch closer, and I sniff the air for scents and roll my eyes. "What the hell are you doing here?"

Calder chuffs, his movements coming to a stop as I sit up and narrow my eyes at him over the back of the couch. "I knew you were fucking here and not in your own damn bed."

"Yep, and I've got dibs on the couch. Too bad. Chair's free though." I grin and know he can see it, even in the dark. Enough natural moonlight is shining in through the sheer curtains.

He groans a little, but steps forward as if to sit next to me. I hoard the throw pillows, holding them to my chest, ready for him to fight me for them. He suddenly freezes, head tilted animalistically to the side as if listening, which has my hackles rising. "Do you hear th—"

Four frantic beeps sound out, indication of the keypad failing, meaning a wrong code was punched in. Heavy breathing echoes on the other side of the door for a split second before Cald's in action, jumping towards the door to open it.

Our omega's on the other side, eyes wide, cheeks flushed, and working too hard to collect air in her lungs. I'm leaping over the back of the couch, there in a heartbeat as Calder urges her into my arms and he runs outside, eyes wild and assessing for any threat. Our alphas roar to the surface, called and prepared to do anything to protect her.

She hugs me tightly, and I pull her up into my arms, wrapping her legs around me. "What's wrong, baby? Talk to me. What happened?" I'm scanning over her features, her trembling body, and note the tear tracks down her pink-tinted cheeks. The sudden urge to hunt, destroy, and maim the unknown threat is overwhelming. I look back and forth between her and the door just as Cald comes back in, shoulders wide and nearly feral.

Stepping closer, I watch him warily, but know neither he nor his alpha would ever dream of hurting her. Scaring her unintentionally?

Maybe. "You good?" I ask him to be sure, and as a little reminder to keep his primal in check.

"Fine." He stalks over silently with a feline grace, gripping her hair and scenting her for any residual scent-stains outside of her fear hanging heavy around her. "What happened." It isn't a question, but a demand, as it comes out rough and with a slight bark hidden in his growl.

"Cald, get a fucking grip," I hiss.

Taking a deep breath, he closes his eyes for a second. When he opens them, they're a little less golden, telling me he's getting his alpha under control. "Sorry, babygirl. Can you tell me what happened? What's wrong?"

" Yes..." She sniffles, lifting her head from my chest and looks up at him, reaching for him. The fact that she's reaching for us when distressed doesn't go unnoticed by either of us, pride filling me from the inside. Taking her from me, he grips her tight, hand wrapped around the base of her neck. "I—Adrian. I met Adrian." Tears start falling freely as she speaks, heartbreak evident through every word. God-mother-fucking-damn-it-to-hell. I clench my back teeth, meeting his eyes, his own anger reflected right back at me, mirroring my own. "He hates me... I didn't even do anything, and he hates me." She starts sobbing, and it breaks my own fucking heart. He's getting a fist to the throat.

She goes on to tell us that she had a nightmare and just wanted some fresh air, and went outside, finding the greenhouse. Turns out, that is where he's been hiding like a fucking coward. In retrospect, it could have been worse, but, he also could have handled it a whole lot fucking better. He's got two pack mates pissed as Hades with him, now. And when Everette learns what he did...

"Why don't we all go to bed, sweet omega? Try to get some rest for a few more hours? We can take some time in the morning to talk more, have breakfast, and we can answer all your questions. We've got you. You're safe. Adrian would never physically hurt you. We'll handle him."

"I have work," she murmurs numbly, a bit out of it.

"I'll handle that too. Don't worry about it. Perks of the family." He winks, but it kind of falls short, a tilted smile on her lips for barely a second.

"Come on, princess."

Warmth envelopes me as we all climb into the small bed, Opaline lying on his chest, and I cuddle up next to them both. Calder rubs circles and strokes her back and hips while I gently massage her temple, head, and jaw. She quickly relaxes. Although the tears seem to fall here and there, as if she's still replaying the moment at random. I try to keep my fingers and my touch soft, but it's difficult with the level of rage I'm trying to smother.

Eventually, her breathing changes, body melting fully on top of Calder, adorable snores puffing out.

"I can't stand seeing her like this, Calder. I'm going to kill him." He forces out a slow breath, but I feel the tension in his body. He's pissed, too, which is oddly a relief. Cald tends to want to understand why people do or say the things they do, especially when it comes to us, always digging deeper, resorting to traumas and triggers and childhood. I normally admire that about him. I really do, and try to be more like him in that sense. But, right now? Right now, I want to tear the skin from his bones and punch the shit out of Adrian with Calder behind me, knowing he has my back.

"I'll handle it, Sage. Okay?" I have a lot I want to say, but bite it back in favor of something more level-headed.

"...That's it? That's all you have to say?" I work to keep my voice even and lighter than I'm feeling.

"Yes. It is. I need time to think this through. It's an incredibly sensitive situation for every single one of us. What do you want me to say?"

"Uh, how about *'Hey, I also want to slam his face into a wall for making our omega cry and walking away like it was nothing.'* His own scent match, Cald."

"Look, I do, alright? Does that revelation make this better suddenly? Admitting my alpha wants to hunt him down for hurting her?" He pauses. "It doesn't. And, I also know that he is not okay, Sage. He needs us."

"I understand that. But, there's no way you're justifying his fucking behavior!" I whisper-hiss, trying not to rock the mattress with my agitation. I know he hears me plenty well; my mouth is close enough to his face.

"Of course I'm not justifying it. Don't give me that shit or that look." He pinches his brows together, glancing over at me before staring straight ahead at the ceiling. "We've known Adrian for years, Sage. He deserves a little grace in this. He never lets anyone in, not all the way. I have no doubt he realized what she is to him, and it scared the shit out of him..."

"Yeah, well," I huff. "He scared her, too. His own omega." We lay in silence for a while. The main sound the rhythmic exploration of

Cald's hands on Opal's back. I finally ask, "Their bond didn't snap into place, did it?" I whisper.

"No. No, I don't think it did. I'm not surprised. Her omega was terrified..." He lingers on his next words. "She was scared when she met us, too. But I think deep down she knew we were safe, letting our bonds solidify immediately. I don't think theirs is going to be solidified until her omega feels safe and cared for by him..."

"I hate this. I feel...helpless. This is the worst possible way this could unfold for her, and I just hate that everything is happening like it is. I want her to be happy. And even though I'm pissed at him, I want him to be happy too. I kind of wish Everette was back, too. She could use some of his natural Xanax, voodoo."

"He'll be back soon, but I agree. As far as Adrian, I think she might be the one other person who can eventually break through to him. I have faith it's going to work out for them both. For all of us. Let me talk to him and handle it for now." Trusting my lead and however he decides to handle this, I grumble, but ultimately agree.

"Sleep. Rest." He adds a hint of a bark in his tone, more of a hard suggestion than a command. Another alpha's bark doesn't affect alphas like it does omegas. But he's my lead, and that holds an entirely different weight.

I don't fight it. Instead, I fall into the gentle bark and let it wash over me, darkness on the edges, as I fall into oblivion.

41

Opaline

A sharp pain in my lower stomach brings me back into the darkness of the room. I realize immediately, with the near suffocating warmth around me, I have my two alphas with me, their giant bodies on both sides, contributing to the darkness. Biting my cheek, I fist my hands, a whimper fighting its way out as I wait for the wave of nauseating pain to pass. Their mingled scents: citrus, amber, and dark liquor mixing with the electric sensation after a snow storm and a hint of coffee blanket me and help keep me grounded.

When my body feels looser, and the pain's mostly gone, I take a silent, slow breath and try to allow my eyes to adjust to the wall of black, feeling a little dizzy and out of it. Their deep breathing is nearly in sync, and a part of me is coherent enough to recognize it's oddly cute. The heat is stifling. I try to push back my hair from my forehead and cheeks, only to realize the strands are wet and my hand is vibrating with tremors. The fog that's still clinging to me doesn't feel like it's entirely sleep. It's them and my sudden need for something only they can give me. Us. My omega is taking the lead, and it finally hits me then with a short-lived moment of clarity.

Of course, it's another heat spike.

Their scents are thick around me, filling my lungs and coating my skin, like I can reach out and feel their fog. I close my eyes and fall deeper into my body and let my omega lead us. Calder's body is wrapped around my back, warm and hard. My appreciation for his utter masculinity and unyielding strength comes out in a whimper. Such a good alpha for me. Perfect. Instinct pushes my hips to rock and move until I'm nestled against the impressive bulge between his legs.

The rough, sleep-laced words that vibrate his chest do nothing to ease the building ache. "Mmm, babygirl. You awake?" I moan, reaching for purchase to help push myself harder against him. Need more.

I vaguely realize I'm also pushing on Sage in front of me, waking him up in the process, too. "Baby?"

"Yeah?" I rub my cheek against the bare skin closest to my face, scent marking, and turn to bite and sink my teeth in.

"Omega—" Calder's bark stops me in my tracks, freezing my teeth from penetrating deeper, stilling my lips. I hate it. The whimpers that leave me now are justifiably and plainly frustration.

"She's burning the fuck up, Cald."

"I know. I can feel the heat of her pussy through the fabric of my boxers," he groans behind me. "Look at me, little omega." I feel his fingers gently on my chin, pulling me away from where my teeth are. Suddenly as a brief few seconds of solid lucidity hit, the realization of my actions shocks me, stealing a gasp. I was just about to bond one of them, biting them and claiming them.

One impulsive second, guided by my omega, would have connected our souls forever.

"I'm sorry. I'm so sorry." I try to scramble back, but all it does is push me harder against Calder's body. Both men speak over the other to reassure me, their soft and kind words an effort to soothe. Falling back under the slight fog, I nod and murmur my agreement, the pulsing need and heat at the apex of my thighs holding all of my attention. The sharpness of pain builds, and I feel myself curling inward, shaking from the intensity as it peaks.

"Alpha." A whine slips free from the hurt.

"We're here. You're having another heat spike, I think, babygirl." I nod, and a series of whimpers leaves my throat as the knife in my lower stomach pushes in deep, twisting. "You want your alphas to take care of you? Make you feel better?"

"Yes." I open my eyes, and the shine of Sage's in the dark flash just enough, I know he's looking at me. "Please?" The word is barely a whisper, but I feel their attunement to me so deeply right now, I have no doubt they both hear my plea.

Sage moves quickly first, throwing the blankets to the bottom of the bed, pushing himself further and further down. Calder pulls up my new nightgown to my waist, exposing me and my slickened thighs, some of the oppressive heat simmering.

"Fuuuck me, sweetheart. Look at this perfect, sweet pussy dripping just for us." His breath skates over my skin as he murmurs more words. Two hands grab my sides, and I'm being rearranged until I'm flat on my back, Sage settling in between my thighs. His shoulders take up so much real estate, my legs find their home instantaneously. The sound of him licking his lips, his breath teasing my skin, sends me into another wave of desperation, rocking what little I can with the hands holding me in place. "Mmm, please, baby. *Pleeaseee,"* he begs in quiet, whispered words in the silence of the night. "Just a taste, princess. Just a taste. Give me permission." I can feel the trembling in his body, the wiggles of effort to stay in place instead of diving in. The groans and need in every movement, every breath of his over my skin, like I can practically feel his tongue reaching and pulling back just before making contact, nearly pushes me over the edge right here.

"Sage, Sage, alpha," I grip his silky, dark hair, trying to move him where I want him. "Need yo—" The words don't have opportunity to leave my lips before his tongue is everywhere: tasting, licking, devouring me.

My hips move of their own accord, thighs shaking as he finds a rhythm, tonguing my clit. He sounds like a dying man finding water in a desert. Between both of our noises, Calder's deep tenor joins, offering rough praise. "That's our good girl. Trusting her alpha to take care of her and this sweet cunt." His lush lips and wet, wandering tongue find their way to my neck, teasing and adding to my aching need for release. The sensation grows in my body, everywhere they touch. "Such a good fucking girl. Our perfect omega." He nips at my earlobe, thick fingers finding my nipple. Torturous circles cause the tips to tighten, the movement mirroring that of his tongue on my ear.

Calder's praise, touch, groans, and attention to my ear and neck, combined with Sage's nonstop, rhythmic licking, tense my body, and I feel myself begging, on the cusp, waiting to fall into my climax. "I—close..." I barely manage the nonsense words, but Sage must understand me, reading my body. His growl echoes in the room, vibrations moving through my thighs and into my clit. He never stops, never changes pace. Just growls deeply, tongue working, and finally, as my breath nearly stops, he shoves a finger inside me, and I break, completely unraveling for them. Calder's praise fills the area next to my ear, his own fingers somehow moving to match Sage's tongue, simultaneously slowing as my peak passes and I start panting and shaking, breathless moans quieting. "Oh my god..."

"We've got you, babygirl. We've got you." Calder's hands trace the length of my sides and down onto my thighs. "Relax, sweet girl," he pushes. I realize how tense my body still is, and I actively let go, legs falling slightly to the sides, arms collapsing.

Sage's warm tongue runs slowly over the insides of my thighs and the sensitive junction of my hips. The closeness of the sensation to my overly-aware downstairs bits makes me whine a little; not sure if I want more or want him to stop. "Want more of your come, princess. Want you to come again."

"Sage, I can't," I say breathlessly.

"Can." He keeps licking, this time landing back on my sensitive clit, and I gasp, knees trying and failing to snap together. "Mmm, mhmm."

The fight quickly fades in me, any response drifting in the wind along with my groans of pleasure. His fingers move at a torturous pace, slowly pumping in and out, curling and hitting the spot I want him most. All I can think about is what it would be like to be filled by my alpha. Connected. Joined as close as we could possibly be. His knot easing the pain deep in me. The thought sends a fresh wave of slick dripping from me, over his hand, his approval more than clear. "Sage...want you...inside me," I whimper the words, the image of him, knot deep, riding me hard, ready to beg. He pauses, and I look down, his eyes practically glowing. We stare at each other for no longer than a few seconds before he releases a snarl that should have concerned me. But it only fuels me more, wiggling and moving, already knowing his next demand.

"Present for your alpha." His words are guttural, far deeper than I've ever heard my sweet Sage. I know without a single doubt that his primal is either in control or fighting him for it. I know I'm safe. Far more than safe. I'm cared for and with my literal soul mates. Nothing could feel more right than knowing we'd be joined, locked together. I need it. Need to know what it feels like to have Sage's knot filling me.

I scramble to get into position, his hands finding my hips. The warmth and heat of his velvet skin barely touches my thighs, and yet it feels like a zap of lightning straight to my core. I can hear how needy I sound, my whimpers and whines begging for Sage to give me what my omega needs. No, what we both need. This isn't entirely my omega leading. Isn't the fog of a heat spike. It's him and me, and everything I'm desperate for. Wiggling my ass in the air, he playfully smacks it. The sounds I'm producing seem to get caught in my throat at the act. Without preemption, my arms stretch in front of me, my face looking to the side.

My eyes find Calder's in the dark, and unconsciously, I reach towards him. Want his skin and his touch on me, too. "Alpha..." I whisper the word, but he catches it, and I hope he knows it was just for him. The look on his face is hard to make out. But I can sense the weight of his sudden emotional turmoil. His doubt that he should be here, feeling like he should leave and give Sage and me this moment. Guilt, even? For what, I have no clue. I don't have the full ability right now to dissect it all. Instead, I simply reach further, grabbing his hand myself.

I can feel my other alpha behind me just before he slips his cock against my wet pussy, an open-mouthed groan escaping him. He rocks back and forth, coating his length in my slick and come. "My omega ready?" he asks, making sure I'm still just as in this as he is. I have no doubts. Need him to mark me and claim me in a primal way that leaves no room for arguing who I belong to.

Nodding, I whine, trying to push back against him. His low chuckle teases, lingering in the nearly-damp air. Melting my fingers with Calder's large ones, I squeeze and never look away, never break our connection as his packmate pushes into me from behind. My mouth falls open, quiet gasps and breaths hovering closely.

Finally, I can feel Sage's swelling knot touch my lower lips. Pausing, he retreats and pushes back in again and again. The stretch is nothing short of magnificent. He reaches places my fingers simply can't, his size and feel nothing compared to any toy or beta I've been with in the past. It isn't just the physical pleasure. It's the fact it's him. It's them.

Pleading towards Calder, I hope he understands that I need him too. That I want him to be in this, be a part of this moment. I need them both so much. Finally, finally, I think I can see dawning on his face in the night. Moving forward, his lips meet mine, his own unique brand of contradiction, both powerful and gentle. He doesn't tease. He devours me as Sage's thrusts increase. Each time his hips land, a new spark catches flame in me. My moans and whimpers tumble into my lead's mouth, his hand gripping my hair at the roots, holding me where he wants me. His tongue dances with mine, nearly stealing my breath. Breaking away from his hold, I look directly into his eyes, begging, "More. Need you, alpha."

There's a split second, I feel he might deny me. The fear barely has time to take root before he's moving and standing on the side of the bed, reaching to help reposition me. With his enormous size, I find myself directly in front of the bulge in his boxers. "You want this, little omega?" His fingers stroke my chin, powerful hands holding my jaw gently.

Sage's hips slow, nearly pausing altogether. I quickly reach for his waistband, pulling the smooth fabric down, realizing there's already precum soaking through. My omega preens at the idea that we please him. His heavy cock bounces free, perfectly towards me. My eyes physically, and I'm sure comically, widen at the sight. Calder isn't just a little bit above average. He's huge. I'm almost positive I audibly whimper at the sight, hesitant. There's no way that's going to fit in me...much less my mouth. "I—" I don't know what to say. I don't want to disappoint him.

Just like the true man he is, Calder leans down until we're face to face again. "Babygirl." I nod and wait for him to continue. "We were made for each other," he sweetly whispers. "Our fate was written in the stars, our bodies designed by the universe to be perfectly compatible. We were made to fit." He's right. I believe in every word he says. They're my perfect matches, my soulmates. And just as importantly, I'm safe in their arms, in this bed. I'm theirs. "I'll go slow, you're in control, little mate. Always. I won't move an inch unless you beg me to." Only Calder, this alpha, could somehow say the perfect thing, know exactly what I need to hear.

Leaning even closer, his lips find my ear, his words just for me. Although I have a pretty good feeling that with their hearing, Sage can pick up on every syllable. "But, when I take you, babygirl. Truly take you and make you mine, you will take every single inch of me like I know you can and squeeze my knot as I fill you and fuck you until not another single drop of my come will stay inside without dripping out." He growls the words, causing my pussy to spasm around his packmate. "You're mine to worship, little mate. Not to hurt."

"Ah, *fuckkk.* Whatever you just said, she likes. Can confirm she fucking likes." Sage groans, sounding less feral and more like himself, moving again, picking his pace up as Calder chuckles darkly and stands again, next to the bed. Cheek in his hand, he traces the delicate bone, landing on my lower lip.

"Take your alphas, babygirl."

42

Calder

My omega is a fucking vision. Every wet-dream come to life.

Watching Sage's cock disappearing in and out of her glistening cunt as her eyes roll is the second hottest thing I've ever experienced. The first is having my tongue on her pussy myself, drowning in her slick.

Every time he pushes against her G-spot or hits deep, her moans vibrate against the head of my dick, and her eyes roll back. My alpha is close to the surface, but I hold a tight leash, keeping myself under control, and staying present. The urge to rut, bite, and claim rides me heavily. When my eyes aren't open, the only images I can see are her presenting for me, pretty pussy dripping, my own cock fucking hard and deep.

I offer her my continuous praise, sweet and encouraging words she seems to love, which was good. Because damn it, if I didn't love me a good girl. It feels a little like relief to know we naturally complement each other in those specific areas, too.

A particularly hard thrust from my packmate pushes her a little further onto my dick, causing her to choke a little. I rush to pull her off of me, but a whine leaves her lips, a couple of tears leaving the far corners of her eyes as she grabs me and eagerly gets back to sucking me off. Having her hot mouth around my sensitive head is like seeing fucking god, kneeling at the gates. The expansive explosion of white overtakes my vision every so often.

"Fuck, princess. I'm not gonna last much longer." I know Sage's eyes are closed due to the lack of a reflective glow, and I have a distinct feeling his mind is bouncing between the present and naming different types of coniferous vegetables.

Gripping the roots of her hair just enough to get her attention, I pull a bit, forcing her eyes to mine. "You want to take our come, omega?" I watch, entranced as she keeps bobbing on my head, hand running the remaining length. "Think you can swallow me down?" Her moans and whines around me, motions speeding up slightly, are all I need to hear and see. "Punish her little clit while you fuck her," I instruct Sage. Even if I could see more than the outline of their bodies, I'd know exactly when his fingers find her sensitive nub with the way her body reacts.

"Fuck, baby. Need to see you come again, princess," he pushes, growl slipping into his words. "I'm gonna knot this pretty pussy and keep you locked on me for the rest of the night, my come filling you." His breathing increases, as does the hastening of his hips. Opaline's eyes shut, taking what he gives her.

Helping her, I tease my hips to match the rhythm of their bodies, taking over so she can focus more on the sensations overtaking her, hand still in her hair. The feel of her hot, warm mouth, the jiggle of her ass and hips as every thrust lands quickly becomes too much. "Gonna come, baby. Take me like a good girl." The distinct pressure and burst of pleasure exorcises my body, a snarl leaving my lips as my come fills and overflows from the sides of her mouth. It takes every ounce of my control to keep my beast leashed so I don't fuck her face. My explosion feels like it sets them off, Sage's groans practically echoing in the small, confined space as he fucks into her, knot hitting its mark in her internal nesting channel. I go to pull out as she trembles and screams around me, but freeze in sensation, tensing myself, as a smaller load spurts from my cock, surprising me. Fuck, my omega just made me come twice in a row.

Finally, in-sync, our bodies loosen, groans quietening. I pull out of her mouth, and she releases me this time, swallowing deeply and collapsing onto her cheek. Sage leans forward, moving as if to reposition her and groans like the movement is too much in his overly sensitive state. I chuckle and bend to help get our sweet girl onto her side. With her dead weight, I realize she's breathing a little heavily. "I... I think you literally fucked her to sleep, Sage," I whisper as he settles behind her, still locked inside her. A fierce jealousy flares momentarily. That insecurity that she wanted him first. I bury it as quickly as I can and hope her well-pleasured omega scent fills his nose enough so that he won't notice the seconds mine had soured.

"I can't believe she's real." His words come out mumbled and slurred, and I realize he, too, is on the verge of passing out, which genuinely makes me fight back a laugh.

I can't help it. I simply stand, staring at the two of them, taking the sight before me in, memorizing it. All the nights spent dreaming of this mystery woman now in our pack, in our arms, in our bed, are reconjured. She's really here. My omega, blissed out and soft, lashes fluttering faintly against shining, flushed cheeks. My packmate, essentially my brother, curls protectively around her, relaxed in a way I haven't truly seen in years, if ever. And me...standing here, somehow a part of this and worthy.

The primal ache still lives inside me, though. That soul deep need to protect her, to be enough for her. My alpha and I want to make her feel so safe, so wanted, so loved, that she'll never again wonder her worth, her value, simply being her. Never wonder or doubt how much we adore her. If I can't do that, what use am I to her or my pack as their lead? I stop the thoughts of Adrian before they land.

I exhale slowly and gently climb back into the bed with them. She moves, even in her sleep, towards me, reaching for me. I curl around her, arm resting over them both, like the protector I was born to be for her, for them.

Burying my nose in her hair, I whisper almost indecipherably, "You're safe, sweet omega. And, you're ours. Forever."

43

Adrian

The heel of my hand pounds against my sternum, bound to leave bruises, all in an effort to force my alpha back into the padded cell I've kept the beast locked away in.

Every part of me is humming with an erratic, electric energy I haven't felt in years. It takes effort to close my eyes, feeling left alone with the chaos inside my own body. My blood thrums, heart pounding with the pressure in my head, and every muscle feels like I've been shot with enough adrenaline to lift a car. At least with my eyes open I can fool myself into believing I'm fully in control and connected to reality.

My alpha snarls and the sound echoes through the space around me, shaking the thin walls as I fight and snarl back to my own primal like a lunatic. The sounds of ceramics and pottery shattering join me in the release.

Fuck, bite, mate, claim.

The words are the world's worst fucking carousel, strong enough that I can nearly feel myself dizzying from the rides around again and again. Can almost see the bright bulbs twirling, overlapping as I see double.

"FUCK."

Fuck, bite, mate, claim.

The continuous pounding of my heart moves south, the unwelcome heat of lust urging me into a fresh spiral. It's an unrecognized level of need turning my cock to steel.

Omega.

Mate.

The growl emitting from my chest pauses with an unbridled purr as a whiff of her lingering scent surrounds my senses.

Sharp pulls on my roots bring me back enough to breathe. Focus. Breathe.

My promise to Calder was useless. My pathetic attempt at never scenting her. I told Calder this wouldn't happen. If I just stayed away, I'd never know, she'd never know. The one fucking place I'm able to find any semblance of peace and solitude...the greenhouse, was suppose to be off limits to her.

The instant I caught her scent, I just...knew. My alpha sure as shit knew. She's mine. My omega. My scent match.

Fated by the universe to be my perfect mate.

Only I had my perfect mate. She died in my arms.

The weight of the overwhelming grief that never quite leaves me wars with the emotion still pumping through me urging me to hunt the new omega and sink my teeth into her neck.

Our bond didn't snap into place.

Even that fleeting thought being my saving grace flies out the window fast. It won't matter. I know that more than most...because I had to, trying to save Natalie.

Proof of my failures as an alpha conjure behind my eyelids. Proof that I don't deserve a chance at another omega.

Natalie and I had fallen for each other before we really knew what love truly meant. She wasn't my scent match, but I never cared. It hadn't even crossed my mind while we were together. She was perfect and was perfect for me. My entire world and future in one person.

Or so I thought.

For months, I watched helplessly as she deteriorated, getting more and more ill in front of my eyes. Nine doctors and none of them knew what was wrong with her. At least that's what she told me.

The truth? The truth was that her father had sold her off in an arranged marriage. She had stumbled upon *him* while he and his own father were visiting, meeting with the piece of shit father of hers. And just like that, the course of our future was forever changed.

They were scent matches. Not us.

Loyal to me and our love, she had refused him and ran. Omegas aren't built to fight their scent matches, their soul bonds. Over time, it breaks them down from the inside out. She fucking knew that. I'm still so god damn angry with her for keeping it all from me. We could have fucking figured it out for christ's sake! Nothing in the entire world, including my own happiness, was worth her life. Nothing.

By the time she decided to tell me, she was too far gone. The damage irreversible. She was terrified that she had waited too long and wouldn't make it. I had to lie to her fucking face, by her bedside day and night, convincing her that she was getting better slowly, even if she couldn't feel it. Because I fucking *knew* and I couldn't bear the thought of breaking her heart with goodbyes, putting the pressure on her of the decisions she made to protect us. What we had.

Within a week, she passed away.

Since then, I've disgraced omegas for it. False blame to an entire designation because I just can't accept it. Need something, someone, other than myself to pin my hatred to, because it had destroyed me enough that it's influence leaked over into other areas of my life.

And, now...my own scent match appears in our lives out of the blue from the void of the fucking universe. And, I know if I deny her after we've scented each other, after awakening a not-snapped-into-place-yet bond, she will die because of me. Not only does that thought make me fucking sick and rageful, it twists a knife in my stomach to know it would affect my pack brothers. They would wither to nothing after losing their soulmate. It's their dream come to life to have a fated omega.

Through the years since I've moved to Mount Fir's Landing and found them, we've not once gone to any of the Omega Care Facility's events or mixers. We never even registered as a pack. Never completed the questionnaires or submitted our scents for their database. There was always some excuse Calder used to protect me from the truth I already knew. It was because of me. Out of respect for my baggage and bullshit.

The emotion clouding my head makes me feel like I'm in another dimension, a ghost just outside of the veil of reality. Thoughts from every angle torment me enough to wish I could rip into my own skin to pull them out one by one until there's nothing left of me.

The longing to have my packmates near me, to have Calder in my ear with his easy reassurances is strong. I know without a doubt though, once he learns I made her cry and hurt her this badly, he won't forgive me. And if he won't, the others most certainly will not. The imagined hatred on Ever's beautiful face brings bile to my throat.

Only now, running isn't an option. I simply can't without committing to the deaths of five people, because I would follow my packmates into the grave.

I can't leave without her being harmed and sliding into the Bonded Illness.

Fuck, god damn it. My alpha saw her, scented her, and went feral. I still feel the chaotic energy pulsing under my skin like sickly glitter around the tornado of emotion and spiraling thoughts. I can't recall having ever been nearly overpowered by my primal. It was *terrifying,* being so close to literally not being in control of my own mind or body.

I fought it, barely, but I'm not sure how long I can realistically keep that up. Because I will have to be near her again.

And...she hates me. As she should. As they all should.

She didn't ask for this, and neither did I. Yet, here we are. Why the fuck would she want me after that pathetic display?

I can still smell her brown sugar and candied honey, feminine twinged musk. My alpha's still prowling under my skin, displeasure at not being near our mate clear.

Opaline... Calder had said her name while we were on the phone. It didn't fit. Not until I saw her. Now, it feels like her, like a perfect fit. She's undeniably beautiful; that isn't a question. Just like an Opal gem.

Banging on my chest to get my alpha in line, I pace and stare at the door, the thought of going after her eating me.

This was not supposed to happen.

Nothing will ever be the same.

44

Opaline

The residual ache between my thighs serves as a constant reminder of how the late hours of the night went for the three of us. Blushing heat warms my cheeks, even in the empty laundry room. They had taken such loving care of me last night. Physically, but also emotionally, after my run-in with my newest alpha. Adrian. The raging fear that morphed into heartache had lived in me for what felt like hours, laying between them. Having them so close, their soft touches and constant calming reassurances was more support than I'd had in an unspeakable amount of years.

The truth was simply that my mate rejected me. He doesn't want me.

Just the thought clenches my jaw, chin wobbling again as tears start to prickle behind my eyes. How I have any left to fall is beyond me at this point. Choking down the sensation, I focus on my surroundings and what I can see, hear, touch, and even smell. Anything to pull me out of the beginnings of another thought spiral.

With the weight of it all though, I'm not alone in carrying this anymore.

I'm not alone.

I trust my lead to do what's best for the pack and to handle the situation, while knowing his support will be unending. Guilt comes and goes at my desperate sadness towards Adrian. I have two amazing mates that have done nothing but show me how devoted they are to me as their omega. To be so upset over an alpha I don't even know and that has only shown to be a feral, terrifying beast feels absurd. Although my feelings are complex with Adrian, the fact remains that he is still my mate. My pull towards him and his alpha will be instinctual and eventually, undeniable. Our bond never snapped into place, which is giving me even more anxiety about the situation than I already have.

Even this morning, Calder and Sage had reassured me over and over, calming my system and my inner primal. We got a quick breakfast, and they dropped me off at the main lodge for my shift, which I somehow managed to still arrive on time for. I appreciate their offer to use their status as the owners to make exceptions for my tardiness with Jewel, but I want to do my best, and being late so early on won't get me there.

A noise from the door catches my attention, rousing me from my thoughts.

"Good lord! It's a monsoon out there!" Lottie pushes her way into the laundry room, a pale green rolling cart behind her. Rushing to help her, I drop the towel that's in my hands and hold the door to the side. "Thank you."

"No problem." Reaching for the discarded fluffy bit of fabric, I hold out the towel for her. Offering her thanks again, she pats her hair, face, and shirt of any lingering water. Most of which had already soaked into her shirt and flattened her pretty hair. Even looking like a drowned rat, this girl is still gorgeous. "Dirty towels, I take it?"

"Yeah, just hauled them over from the spa. They're fully booked. Rainy days here always drive guests to the spa for treatments. Trying to help as much as I can, and they're already low on clean, getting a little frazzled."

"Understandable. Well, I have a whole new cart of their table bedding and towels ready to go! Want me to take them over?" I step closer to the table and pull the cart by the corner, wheeling it over.

"Nah, no sense in both of us getting soaked." She grins, like being drenched is no big deal. Looking around, she does a once-over of the space before leaning against the wall, hands clasped. "How's everything going? Settling in okay?"

"Honestly, yes. It's been incredible here, a saving grace. I wasn't doing too hot before coming here." I pause, the fear-based and conditioned part of me telling me to stop, to not give her any more information than is necessary to finish the conversation. The other part of me, desperately hoping for friendship, wants to trust her deeply. "Um, but, yeah. A lot of dreams I gave up on a long time ago are somehow close to coming true. I'm overwhelmingly thankful and also a little scared," I joke.

Instead of what I'm expecting, she smiles softly, like she understands. And, it's genuine. I wonder if maybe there is more to this woman than meets the eye. It's easy to judge people blessed with pretty faces and good genetics, assuming their lives have been easier. But that just isn't fair. Being pretty doesn't stop abuse, doesn't prevent a poor childhood, and doesn't demand that you receive love. It's a biased assumption on my part.

I quickly realize it isn't far off from the assumptions on life as an omega. We're all taught, every designation, that omegas are sought after, the center of packs, what our biology depends on to continue growing our lineages. There's a constant hatred between omegas and a lot of beta women simply because, at the heart of it all, we all want to feel special, sought after, and dream of soul mates. Betas, by nature, would never have that chance to find a scent match. Their biology is just different enough from alphas and omegas that scent matches aren't a thing. Thus, over the years creating a divide between designations.

Not all betas feel the same. Lottie, for example, is one of them, clearly. She seems compassionate, kind, and genuinely a good person. I know she understands what I allude to on a level I may never learn the details of.

"I know it may seem scary, especially if you're going through a lot of change all at once. But that's what a rebirth is, isn't it? A death of the old you, making way and providing space for a new you, new blessings to come in." She leaves her place against the wall and steps towards me. "You absolutely deserve all the happiness life is blessing you with. And, if no one else has told you yet, your alphas are wonderful people. They care deeply about the town, their resort, and creating a healing space for everyone, and go out of their way to take care of their staff. Truly. So, I don't know if that really helps ease any fears or not. But it's the truth. You can trust them. We all do."

Swallowing deeply, I barely manage to offer her a nod with an emotion clogging smile.

"Want a hug?" She asks, opening her arms and tilting her head in a playful way.

"How could I say no?" We embrace each other, and it feels comfortable and somehow healing for a different part of me. Having my alphas is the biggest gift in life I could have ever hoped for. But, this? Friendship? It's a gift entirely in and of itself. "Thank you, Lottie. It's been nice getting to know you, to make a friend here, ya know?"

"I do!" She pulls away, and it's like the bubble of her peaceful, yet happy nature, moves and floats with her. "I have a couple of girlfriends in town. We'd love it if you wanted to maybe join us for our next girls' night! Nothing crazy," she chuckles. "But, we have a good time."

"I would love to join..."

"You got it!" She clasps her hands together against her chest out of excitement. "There's also the Mountain Glow Festival coming up, too! The guys put it on every year for the locals, mostly." Peeking at the window behind me, her brows raise, speaking again before I can ask questions. Whatever it is, it sounds nice. I'm curious to hear more about the Festival. "Hey, I'll see ya around though. It looks like there's a break in the rain, and I gotta get back to work. I'll probably be back to drop off more laundry. Wish me luuuckkk!" She adds a little sing-song lilt to the end of her sentence and turns with a big wave before leaving.

Even after the door closes and the quiet of the room leaves everything still, I smile at the interaction.

I have a real friend.

45

Opaline

The day's gone by quickly. I genuinely love the repetitive nature of the work I'm doing. It allows me to zone out and even listen to audiobooks that they had set me up with on the phone. Between that, keeping my hands busy, and the guys stopping by to check on me again and bring lunch, it's feeling like a great day. Although I'm not sure what the evening will hold for me. We haven't discussed any plans. The rain's stopped, too, at least from what I can tell from inside. Lottie's been in and out a few times, as well as the general manager checking in to make sure everything is going okay, and I don't have any questions. Overall, I'm feeling better.

Opening the windows, a fresh breeze circulates the room, cleansing the air as it comes and goes. The humid air carries the scents of the nearby spring pools and refreshing magic that follows a rainstorm. Humming a little, my hands work, stacks of perfectly folded towels and low rows of sheets taking up the expanse of the tabletop.

The somehow distinct character voices from the same narrator keep me so entranced, I'm startled when someone new comes through the door; an entirely new face...

"Oh! Hello. You must be new here. I'm Pack Morrison's house attendant." The dark-haired woman reaches out her hand to shake mine, parking a small wagon-esque bin behind her.

"Uh, hey. Sorry, I wasn't expecting anyone else to be stopping by. Is there anything I can help you with?" I offer, taking her hand, skipping the introductions. I don't entirely know what a house *attendant* is, but something about her rubs me the wrong way immediately.

"No problem at all. I was actually just dropping off the guys' laundry."

The...guys'...laundry... My omega puffs up, nearly forcing me to growl at the woman. She's handling and touching my alpha's clothing, their bedding, her scent infiltrating their lives. I hate the very thought, but...I have no right to feel this way. Of course, they had lives before I suddenly came into it. They've all had lovers, history, and now, a house attendant. My jealousy and overwhelming, sudden insecurity are something I have to learn to manage. Objectively, I am aware of my ridiculous feelings.

"What does that mean?" I ask a little tartly, before clearing my throat to add, "I'm new, I'm still learning." Two thoughts fight for dominance in my brain. One, this woman has done nothing to deserve my vitriol. She simply has a job, and she is trying to do it. The other, is to make it known that they are my alphas, my scent matches, my soulmates. To stake my claim and make it obvious to any women in their lives. Or anyone who even looks at them, for that matter. The growl still holds itself in my throat, but I try to bury it, leaning into my logical side. Not my primal.

"Oh, sure... um, well basically, I just bring their laundry here so that it can be done in bulk and pick it back up once it's done if they're not able to."

"And you clean their house?" I can tell she's a little put off by my tone and my questions. I curse and kick myself for being so fucking rude. But, my primal has a chokehold on me, I just can't free myself from. I wonder if last night's conflict is still lingering and affecting me on a deeper level.

"I do...normally once or twice a week. I've been doing it for several years." She kind of trails off slowly, as if considering, thinking. "Are you okay?" Fuck. That's the punch in the gut I need. The fact that I'm behaving this way makes me a little nauseous. I'm not this person, this woman, this omega. I hate this behavior when it's me being given the treatment. I can feel my shoulders slump physically as my omega takes a backseat.

"I'm sorry. I just..." I realize then that I have no idea if they're telling many people about me and the fact that I'm their scent match. I have no right to go blabbing it myself, do I? But the embarrassed part of me feels like I need to divulge a reason for my petulant actions. "I'm nearing my heat, and my primal is closer to the surface than usual. I'm sorry," I explain.

Her eyes nearly roll, body language changing in an instant. My shoulders tense, jaw following, a little too much to be comfy. "Ah, got it. Best of luck," she deadpans. "Anyway, here's this. Let the front desk know when it's ready, and they'll handle pick up with either Pack Morrison or me." Turning to leave without another word, she steps through the doorway, the door closing softly behind her. So, my instinct was a little bit correct on my initial read on her. She clearly has some form of ill-will against omegas. That doesn't necessarily make her a bad person, though. Just not someone I should or would like to be close to.

It's completely unjustified and illogical, but I can't help but start to imagine myself in her place. I can be the one to take care of the household. The images flood me, enough to lean against the table to hold myself upright: days waking up and cooking breakfast, snuggling in a nest, movie nights, ice cream, simply existing in the same shared space, building a life.

But that can't happen. Not only am I not quite there just yet. But Adrian hates me for unknown reasons. I know he lives with them; he's their packmate. I can't bear the thought of being a cause of tension between them either. I trust Calder to handle the situation fully. I have to.

Suddenly, the day feels a bit more heavy with things I clearly need to sort out. Another topic that needs to be addressed is, in fact, my heat. I know it's coming. They know it's coming. And, simply put, it needs to be put out in the open and planned for. The truth is, I'll be under the fog of my heat and begging for their knots, begging them to impregnate me. Even if it's not what I want. My omega will be in control, me in the backseat, half aware of what is actually happening. And, the very real possibility of me begging for their bites and their teeth in my neck to claim me is another thing to be talked through. I'm not ready for that either. Not right now. I know I want them forever, am falling for them so quickly. Whether or not it's simply biology and the fact we're mates, or if it's them. Deep down, I know it's probably a little of both.

The pull between alphas and their omegas is undeniable. It's a tidbit of information I was hoping would give me a little more peace than it realistically does regarding Adrian and our nonexistent relationship.

Sighing, I pull the wagon-ish bin she had left over towards the washers to sort and get the loads going. I had also taken care of a couple of items of my own limited clothing. It isn't like I'm doing anything wrong. Lottie had explained there's a set of two smaller washers and dryers in the far corner, specifically for staff use, so it won't interfere with any laundering the resort needs. It's available for our use. It isn't that.

It's a shame I carry that I don't want to be caught with such dirty clothing. I don't want to be stopped on my walk in or caught putting things into the machine, the overwhelming scent buried into the fabrics floating to anyone's nose. So, I had brought one outfit I could have on hand and washed it this afternoon, making a quick trek back to my quarters.

I don't want my alphas to even associate me with that version of myself. The one without water or a home. I can't bear it. I want them to see me for who I want to become, who I want to work towards being for them. Not only for them, but for myself too. So, the fact that I have something I can throw on that isn't their oversized huge clothing feels really good. It lifts the heaviness in my chest that's been residing there too long.

The lid opens from the center, each of the two pieces folding to its own respective side. There are four cream-colored, heavy-duty cloth bags that are tightened and held in place with a small piece of plastic that grips the drawstrings in place. I can safely assume that each holds their own owner's clothing inside.

My body freezes, hands stilling, realization hitting.

They each hold their owner's clothing inside... *All* of my alphas' clothing...

Jumping into action, I fumble, energy renewed, and make work of each bag to open and scent them, frantically pulling at strings and bringing the first bit of fabric to my nose. There's one in particular that I'm looking for, though.

Each one hits me: Calder's frosted pine and coffee... Sage's citrus and amber whiskey... Adrian's fresh rain and cedar wood...

Finally, I reach the last one. I pause, knowing it's him. My last mystery alpha. My hands violently shake, emotion clogging my throat, and tears lining my eyes.

If this man is my scent match, my pack will be complete. No matter our dynamic or the horrific, uncharted waters between Adrian and me, still...it would be us. I would be a part of them.

My pack.

46

Opaline

Time slows, the world nearly tipping and sending me into a dizzy spell.

Anything past the bag and string in front of me fades to nothing as I pinch the small protrusion from the plastic holding his scent from me.

It's not fear that weighs me down, but it's the closest feeling I can compare this level of overwhelm to as my mind blanks and loses all thought but one.

With a snapping pull, it hits me.

The first time your face feels the heat and brilliance of the sun after a long and dreary winter.

Waking up on a lazy weekend morning to creme-filled pastries and sweet coffee.

Vanilla...cinnamon...almonds.

His scent explodes around me.

There is no fighting my omega. We both know this is it. Collecting the soft, dark blue fabric to my nose, I start to collapse, everything pushing up under my skin, rising to the surface and vibrating through me, pouring out of me. The distant, barely-aware part of me prays the door stays in place and no one walks in at this moment.

Releasing it all, unbidden sobs wrack my body, knees hitting the hard floor. I hold the sweater to my nose, tracing and rubbing it across my cheeks and neck, clenching it against my chest.

Mine. My alpha.

But it isn't just that. It's like the final piece of that puzzle is slid into place after all the edges and center pieces, all hugging together harmoniously. The long awaited final stroke of a brush on a canvased painting. It's the moment I know I was waiting for.

Everything about this alpha is home, comfort, love, and gentleness. I just know. There is no explaining it. He will be my safe space, my warm blanket on hard days, soft and lazy kisses on sunny days. It's everything I dream of. A confused part of me wonders why this scent, above Calder's and Sage's is having such a strong effect on me. Every cell in my body screams for him, now.

I don't want to wait for him to return. I want them to call him now and *demand* he come home to meet me, to wrap me in his arms while wearing this exact soft, cozy sweater. I have no idea what he looks like, and I know it won't matter; it doesn't matter. This is my alpha.

I can't explain the feeling, and the guilt is not lost... Truly it has nothing to do with them or how wonderful Calder and Sage are.

But *this* is the mate I've been waiting for, the one I need.

47

Calder

"You know I can't understand you when you speak all at once, right?" I ask.

The sun's muted from the tinted windows of our SUV, a pleasant cool air flowing through the seat under me and directly from the vents ahead. While waiting for Sage, Dad's name popped up on my screen, requesting a video call. I accepted, to which my mom's face now fills the screen, my three pack fathers crowding around her, all speaking at once. It's a sight to behold, to be sure.

I look over their smiling faces, Mom's graying long hair hanging over her shoulder. Rem's closest somehow, his huge shoulders and chest taking up most of the right side of the screen.

"Love, why don't we prop up the phone so we don't all have to crowd around trying to squeeze into a tiny rectangle?" Leon suggests, trying to grab the phone, moving it enough to make anyone seasick.

"Well, I know. I just wanted to see my baby's face up close first. Hi, honey bunny!"

"Hey, Mom," I smile. "Miss you guys."

"We miss you too. Sorry, we didn't get to see you boys, when you dropped into town..." She gives me a pointed look, the moving screen finally settling as Leon sets it up somewhere, the group of them further away. When the smile breaks out on her face, hands clasped in front of her like an excited pup, I know I won't be waiting long for the Opaline questions.

Unable to fight my own dopey grin, I rest my weight on the center console, nodding and waiting for her to blurt out whatever is stewing in that head of hers. "Let's hear it," I chuckle.

"You have an omega! *Calder Elowen Morrison!* You found your *scent match* of all things, and I hear it from your father, and don't hear from you for days!"

"I know, Mom... I'm sorry. I really am. Things have been... well, it's been a lot of change very quickly, and a lot is still working itself out."

"How is the little thing doin'?" Rem chimes in. He was the one to find her behind the pub. In all honesty, I owe him everything. He is the reason my dreams came true. Who knows how or if Opal and I would have even crossed paths otherwise.

"She's actually doing amazing, Dad." I shake my head a little, more in disbelief, still trying to fully comprehend it all. "You have no idea how thankful I am that you took a chance and took care of my omega when she needed it most. I will always be in your debt for that, Rem." I scratch my chin with my thumb a little, thinking and considering where to even begin.

"Is she all settled? Did she still want to work at the resort? How'd the nest turn out? Fill me in!" Mom interrupts. Remi just plays with the ends of her hair as Leon stands behind her with his hands on either shoulder, gently massaging. Zen stands on her other side, elbow propped against the back of the chair she's sitting in. My mother is the center of their universe. Their sun, their moon, their reason for existing. It's the reason I've always dreamed of meeting my fated mate. I've seen what love can look like at its best.

"She is. She is getting settled. Although she did decide that she wanted to take some time to be on her own. So she's staying over in the staff lodging building at the resort. She hasn't moved in the house yet." Mom makes a face of understanding, but her hands drop a little as if maybe a little disappointed. "Honestly, I respect her decision. It was a huge deal for all of us to suddenly find our scent match without expecting it or actively courting. Our pack wasn't even registered with the O.C.F. It was overwhelming in a lot of ways for Sage and I. I can only imagine what it had to have been like for her, especially coming from the harsh environment she had been pushed into." I sigh heavily. "She's the strongest person I've ever met. Literally, my dream come true."

Each of their faces reflects exactly what I would expect. Nothing but utter support, understanding, and love. I've gotten incredibly lucky with the family I was born into, was incredibly blessed to have found my pack mates, and now, the universe has given me the greatest gift an alpha could hope for. I will never not be grateful for the people in my life everyday.

Before any of us speak, the door to my right pops open, letting sunlight in and a warmer breeze. Setting the bag down at his feet, he looks over and notices the phone propped up against the tilted front window. Mom beats him to a greeting, nothing but love for her other adopted son. "Is that Sage? Hi, sweetie! How are you? We were just talking about your omega! Congratulations! I'm so happy for you. I can't wait to meet her! Maybe for that festival you boys put on, we can make the drive up! Wouldn't that be so fun?"

"Take a breath, sweet girl..." Zen chuckles, urging her to slow down, each word tripping over the next.

"Oh, you behave. I'm fine." She bats at his arm playfully, and I can damn near see my own future twenty or thirty years from now.

"Uh, hey, Mom! I'm the best I've ever been in my life if that tells you anything. You'll meet her soon, don't worry. Just need a little more time for us all to get settled," Sage responds with a smile, leaning over to be in the frame.

"We understand. We're thrilled for you and can't wait to meet her and see you boys again. Be good to her. I'm just so happy and excited to watch your relationship grow and evolve. You all deserve a complete family and all the happiness in the world."

"Thank you, Mom. We appreciate it. We're excited too."

"How is Adrian doing with all of this? Is he...settling okay, too?" Remi asks.

Sage and I share a look that must be telling enough from the head shakes and pity that's clear even through the tiny screen. "He's struggling to be honest. His plan was to not scent her, to avoid the inevitable. You know as well as I do that's not how it works. They were destined to meet, and it was only a matter of time. Although I will say it happened much faster than we expected it to."

I push out a quick, deep breath, rubbing the back of my neck to relieve the stress I'm carrying. "She was exploring and stumbled upon the greenhouse, which turns out to be where he'd been hiding from us all. They scented each other, he lost his shit, primal taking control, and frankly, was an asshole. She had no idea what was happening or what she had done wrong. She was in tears and whining for hours afterwards. To say Sage and I are pissed would be an understatement."

"Oh, hell. That poor girl. She didn't deserve that," Zen says, concern clear.

"No. No, she did not... She seems to be doing better today—"

"Don't worry, we took extra special care of her, Cald and I." I throw him a *'what the fuck, seriously'* look at his wink, jaw hanging loose. "Sorry... I mean, we did, though. Intimacy is important between omegas and their alphas!" Closing my eyes I try to reign in my anger and slight embarrassment.

"He's right, you know! Oh don't look at me like that, Calder. Sometimes it's the best way to show your love and affection and take care of her."

I glance at my mom and gape a little. "I can't have this conversation with you, even at this age. I'm sorry." I wave my hands out between myself and the screen as if I can push the lingering words away.

"Sh—"

"I swear to god, Sage. If you say another word, I'm ending this call right now." He only rolls his eyes exaggeratedly and shrugs, miming his fingers like there's a zipper closing and locking his lips shut.

"Anyways, as I was saying... she's doing better today. I think she's just... Not scared, but, confused, hurt, and anxious when it comes to him. I'm trying to be understanding. Sage and I have talked it through and know where we stand. He's our pack brother; we will not abandon him. But, I also will not stand to see my omega clinging to me, whining in her sleep because he hurt her."

"So, Adrian knows then? It's confirmed they're scent matches, too?" Leon asks.

"I'm positive he knows based on the reaction he had. I wanted to get my thoughts sorted and organized before approaching him for a conversation, though. On top of giving him room to work through this on his own first. But, he's spiraling. I can just feel it."

"I think a part of him is still grieving in his own way. Guilt can rot a man's instincts, especially if he's loved and lost an omega before. That intense pain doesn't ever fully go away."

"No, I know. I would agree with you, Zen. And I've given him space, and I've been understanding and mindful of his past." I swipe my hand through my hair, tugging a bit at the roots. "But...their bond is calling to them both now. It didn't snap into place, which I'm not surprised by at all, given the situation. Her omega never had a second to feel safe with him. It's going to keep burning under his skin until he fixes it. He'll eventually go feral if he tries to push her away, his primal permanently taking over. But, what I'm really concerned with..."

"Is her... He's hurting her. She'll get sick and has the chance of death if they're not near each other. Recognition bond or not, they're still scent matches." Mom has tears in her eyes as she brings a hand to cover her mouth, wrapping her mind around this.

"Exactly," Sage answers, tongue tracing his teeth in anger and distaste.

"I will not ever let that happen. Ever. Understand me, Sage?" I grab his shoulder, giving him the touch I know he needs to stay grounded and not get swept up in the tornado of thought that this particular topic can wind into. "I will do anything and everything, including die myself before she gets sick or worse. Not happening." A nod is my response, and that's good enough for me. Looking back at the screen, all of my fathers have their chins lifted or approving looks resting on their faces. I can't say it hurts to know I have their support on this, too. "This cannot go on, though. I have a feeling deep down she believes she's the problem."

"Has she expressed as much?" Zen presses.

I sigh, considering how much I want to divulge. Luckily before I have to, Rem jumps back in. "This is his job to face this head on, not her job to fix it."

"I know. Believe me, okay?"

Mom clears her throat, wiggling a little in her seat anxiously. "Maybe it's time you boys remind him what he wanted all those years ago? The pack, the home, the alpha he wanted to be again. It sounds like he might be reverting under the stress. I know finding his scent match wasn't something he explicitly wanted...but."

"I mean... You're right." Adrian arrived at the resort for seasonal work, grieving and a fucking mess, years ago. We knew he was pack. At some point, finding his footing and his place with us, we learned that he just wanted a pack and a place that felt like home again. He got those things. "Having our omega is only going to make that ten times better. But, to him, Opaline feels like a death sentence."

"Calder, listen to me." Remi grabs my attention, the lead energy in every line of his face, every muscle in his body. I know it well and recognize it immediately on an unconscious level. "You can't force his heart open. But you can remind him that when it does, he won't be alone in it. Because, truthfully, I have no doubt that little omega is going to break his heart open faster than any of you realize. And when that happens, he's going to need you all."

"I hear you, pops. I know you're right." Sucking in enough air to fill my lungs, I take in every word, but clear my head and some of the weight from the conversation. "I think we're going to hop off here. But thank you for everything. You'll meet her soon, Mom. Promise."

"Anything you could need our help or support with, please let us know. Anything, any questions, advice; we're here for it all. Love you, boys. Bye bye."

A chorus of goodbyes echoes over the others as I end the call, picking up the phone.

"Jesus. That turned into something deeper than I expected." I pinch between my brows, massaging lightly. "Anyway, did you find what you were looking for?"

Sage doesn't entirely respond, eyes half-glazed and distant, clearly not wholly present in the vehicle anymore. He nods extra slowly, biting on his lower lip, and looks out the window, brows furrowed.

We have a long road ahead. But, right now, all I want to do is see my omega.

48

Sage

So, let's recap.

Everette is off the grid doing silent Everette things, Adrian's being an asshat with twisted man-panties, and Calder's silently carrying the weight of the world trying to be our level-headed leader. That leaves me...? Somewhere in between, I suppose.

Not perfect.

What is perfect? My omega that lives in my head twenty-four-seven.

Doubt's been trickling in like a faucet in the Winter. Thoughts dripping and pinging against metal, stealing my attention. Of all of us, I'm the least capable of taking care of Opaline like she needs and deserves, especially with my shameful past she doesn't know of yet. How can someone who's never known perfect, give her perfect in return?

What's worse? Even through the gallons of doubt overflowing the sink, any urges to keep her haven't lessened a single bit. If anything, they've only gotten stronger. I'm selfish, aware I don't deserve her, and yet I'm determined to keep her anyway. It's a battle to keep my feelings under wraps, to not tell her how badly I've dreamed of finding my mate, not pushing her too far too fast. I feel like fate's connected us with a delicate thread and if I tug too hard it'll snap and I'll lose her. What I really want to do is braid the thing, wrap it around her, and pull hard enough she lands in my lap, forever.

Ultimately, I want to be the reason she feels safe, can trust again, and has hope for her future. Give her the reassurance that I will wait, no matter how long it takes to claim her and tie our souls together. I want it all with her. I know it hasn't been long by any standard, but scent matches are destined. She's my perfect other half.

I also hope Ever's spaceship lands soon and Adrian pulls his head out of his ass so we can be together as a pack. All of us.

Bulky fingers relying heavily on autocorrect, I type away on my phone, the evening's goal in mind.

It's been like... a few hours since you've seen me

but I miss you too...

I do a stupid little shimmy dance, grin eating my face. She misses me, too.

"What the hell was that?" Calder scares the shit out of me coming out of nowhere, into the kitchen. Luckily, he doesn't catch my flinch. If he does, he doesn't call me out.

"Don't be a hater because I have moves and I get to take our omega out on a date."

"Have you talked to her? How is she?" He reaches for his back pocket, as if to text her at the same time he's asking the same questions he's gonna ask her.

"She seems okay enough, given the circumstances. I haven't even asked her yet, so don't...just, can you wait to text her, please?" My voice gets louder as each syllable slips free, stressing my point.

"How do you know I was going to text her?"

"Wow, Cald. Anyway..." My lashes flutter, raising my brows a little pointedly. "Shush, will you?" I need to focus and text her back.

Any chance I can steal you tonight? Just you and me?

Steal me, huh? Is this where you hide me away for yourself?

Don't tempt me sweetheart...

I have something in mind. Trust me?

I do, very much. I'd love to spend the evening with you.

"You should see your face. I'm saving this as blackmail."

I look up at a phone pointed at me. Rolling my eyes, I flip him off. "Sorry, I'm obsessed with my omega. You're just jealous." I mean it as a tease, but, there's a flash of something that darkens his eyes for a moment. Long enough no one else would have caught it outside of our pack. Before I can manage to say anything further, his smile is back in place. It just doesn't reach his eyes like before.

I kick myself, wondering what the fuck I said. I didn't mean anything by it. Is he actually jealous? Maybe I should invite him to come? The more I think on it, the more I think I should. I would love alone time with her, but, I also need my pack mate to be just as happy as me. I didn't like that flash of a haunted look in his eyes, whatever the hell it was. "You wanna come with tonight? More than enough room. Was going to take her out to the event field. Have a little movie night?"

"Nah, thanks though. I've had my solo date with her. You deserve to have intimate time alone to solidify your relationship and spend time together," he smiles.

"Sure. Well, if you change your mind, just text us. Seriously. I mean... I did technically crash your solo with a cuddle puddle." I forgot I did that and can't help the shake of my shoulders, laughing as I say it. That was kind of a jerk move on my part. I couldn't help it at the time; I was so desperate for her. I still am, though, honestly.

"If I had anyone else to bet that night, I could have won thousands with how confident I was you were going to show up," he says, reaching for a sparkling water from the fridge. I just narrow my eyes with a playful growl as he laughs over his shoulder, heading into the living room.

Can't wait, baby. Wear something comfy. Even pjs or some of our clothes. I have everything covered.

You'll end up curled up next to me. Sooo something you wanna be cuddled in.

There may or may not be blankets involved. And unhealthy snacks. And me trying very hard to not pounce on you.

What if...

I want you to pounce on me?

My throat forgets how to function and perform the one job it's supposed to, sending me into a sputtering cough as I choke on my own spit, hacking like a man dying.

"Jesus, you good?" Cald yells from the couch across the open space, mild concern etched in between his brows.

Nodding, I offer him a thumbs up, residual grit preventing me from breathing normally without coughing. Holy *fuck*. I was not expecting that response. Seems our little omega isn't as innocent as she looks.

Then I will absolutely pounce. Respectfully. And maybe with a little whipped cream.

Be ready in an hour princess. I'll come straight to you.

Ah, fuck. That image wastes no time traveling straight to my dick. Her supple, soft, pale skin...whipped cream on her neck...nipples...stomach...lower. *Fuuuck* me. Flashbacks hit me hard enough that I have to close my eyes and lean against the countertop, trying to stop myself from moaning or humping the air like a feral beast.

"Fucking hell, Sage! Keep it in your pants. I can scent you from over here. What the hell is happening in that conversation?"

"Fuck you. No, actually, I'd prefer to fuck our omega. So, pass. And it's secret." I push off the table and head towards the stairs. "Love you though!"

My nailbeds are a little worse for wear. Dropping my hands, I give myself another once-over in the mirror. Nothing crazy, no button-ups or anything. I told her PJs, so I wore the same. Sweatpants and a snug t-shirt, so she can see how strong I am. My arm flexes in the mirror, proving my point.

Anxiety tickles like pissed off ants under my skin. I don't know why I'm so nervous. I mean, shit, we were fully intimate for the first time just last night. That's normally the biggest thing to be nervous about in a new relationship. I'm just desperate to impress her. I don't know if that's the best word to represent the weight of what I'm feeling. I have to make her feel good, special, give her a night to remember for our first date. She deserves so much, and I want to be able to give her everything she could ever dream of. I can't fail at this.

Closing my eyes, I try to center myself, taking deep breaths like Cald always tells me to, to slow the gremlins in my head. Focusing on the images of Opaline's smile, the way she melts in my arms, and her peaceful face when she's sleeping. It does exactly as I hope, and I already feel better. Because she's my ultimate match. I have nothing to worry about when I'm with her. Just being together and scent-swapping is enough.

Fixing the small, dark curls lingering on my forehead, I smile softly with a final puffed exhalation, and turn to head downstairs.

Walking through the open space that connects our kitchen and living room, I notice Cald's gone, the space dimly lit with soft orange lighting, TV off. Probably in his bedroom. The thought to say bye strikes, but I'm too eager to see our girl. Two pink, glittering gift bags sit by the door waiting for me to grab as I walk out.

Finally, a courting gift for her just from me. My alpha practically puffs up at the thought we're providing for her.

Opening the door, the evening air hits, a small chill in the air, and I can't help practically skipping down the stairs. "Perfect weather for cuddles."

49

Calder

The words on the cream paper fail to register, supposed sentences nonsensical gibberish that require my attention multiple times. I'm only half aware. The soft whisp of pages turning every few seconds, distantly, is a white noise as my hand moves out of habit. Of course, I snap back to the room and go back a few pages. Only to then do the same fucking thing. I've been trying to read this book for over a week and have gotten quite literally nowhere with it. Every night I've not had the blessing to be with my omega, I've collapsed into bed and reached for it from the nightstand, as I normally do. A poor excuse of a distraction from my mind, desperate for the feel of her against me, safe in my arms. Dreams of claiming her with my bite, connecting our souls permanently, are frequent.

I'm happy for Sage and Opaline both. They deserve so deeply to find happiness in one another. They need this time to learn to be comfortable alone together, get to know each other, and add that essential supporting layer to their foundation; our foundation. But would I rather be here lying with her on my chest? Absolutely. The answer will always be yes.

Sage plays up the goofy idiot character at times. I believe part of him sees himself as such, so it's probably not much of a stretch for him, but Sage is so far from stupid. He's incredibly creative, insightful, and is the first to put people at ease with his unique, playful energy, not taking everything too seriously. His home life before my folks took him in was exceptionally rough. I'm hoping more time with her alone will reinforce some self-confidence where he needs it.

The book snaps shut with a soft echo, my hands pressing the sides together as I look around my room, releasing a breath. Still getting used to it. I recently did a bit of a remodel to my private quarters. I hadn't been sure about the dark green that the guys suggested. But it turned out beautifully. The dark wall behind my bed stands out in stark contrast now against the light warmth of the others. New sconces and lighting completely transformed the room, too. The rest of the space is soft wood and touches of other shades of green and warm neutrals. Modern, but not *too* modern.

I'm glad I made the changes. I hope Opaline likes it. I can't wait for the time to come when she wants to settle into her nest, make the space cozy and her own. With her heat undoubtedly coming soon, I worry we won't have time to make everything as perfect as I'd like it to be. That's another conversation to be had; one of many on my list, it would seem. The thought that she may not want to even have her heat here strikes. A lot is happening sooner than we'd imagined, while other things we'd anticipated haven't yet come to pass. Our internal timelines are putting pressure on all of us, whether we realize it consciously or not.

But, if she hasn't even set foot in our home, worried about keeping the peace with Adrian, I assume she may not want to spend her heat in a new, unfamiliar place. Even if our scents are embedded into every fiber and fabric of the huge space, it won't be enough to comfort her omega when she's under the fog of her heat. Understandably. It could be days, weeks, or even months until her heat hits, though, given the situation with Adrian. Will her inner omega and biology fight her heat cycle until our pack is officially settled?

I can't help but worry about the medical implications that could have on her. The heat spikes she's experiencing may be uncomfortable for her, but, I believe they may be better than a far worse alternative, for now.

The house is quiet entirely, save for the occasional owl outside and the soft hum of the air circulating through the vents. Needing the distraction, I reach again for the book to get out of my own head for a while.

I stare blankly at the print, not even pretending I'm absorbing the words this time. Groaning a little, I lean forward, bedding moving with me. Just as I'm about to toss the book to the side and get out of bed, I hear something from deep downstairs. Not one of the many familiar noises our house produces or critters outside. No...the unmistakable sound of the front door. My brows furrow, listening for more; any inclination of which of my packmates it could be. Or, someone else entirely. Removing the covers, I move stealthily towards the door. My ears strain, hyper focusing.

On first assumption, I guess it's Adrian finally fucking coming home and not hiding in his greenhouse, but a quick second later, I wonder if perhaps it's Sage and Opaline. Maybe he convinced her to come back to the house tonight, the chill of the evening as we move into the new season too much for their date. I try to dampen the excitement that bubbles up surprisingly at the thought, ready to rip the handle off the door to get to her quicker. Either way, I need to be downstairs.

The further I get down the hallway and start down the stairs, I realize it can't be Opaline. Nothing in my chest that lights up when she's near, naturally triggering my instincts, so much as stirs. Heavy footsteps echo in a pattern, enough to reach my ears. Pacing.

It's Adrian then.

Taking a deep breath, I center myself and prepare for the war, the battle, I'm likely about to step into.

Just before turning the corner, a glance down the remaining stairs reveals a shadow stretching along the hardwood. From the angle, it's a safe guess that the track lighting on the bottom of our upper cabinets is on, Adrian pacing behind the island. I purposefully add weight to my steps nearing the bottom to let him know I'm coming.

Chest inflating in a final attempt in preparation for this conversation, I round the corner, shock and surprise bringing me to a freezing halt.

Not Adrian.

Standing in our kitchen barefoot, hands in his curly brown hair, he paces like a caged animal, fighting some internal battle. Turmoil is clear on his normally serene expression, evident in the tension lining what should be a relaxed and rested body. Glancing over, I see his luggage thrown by the door haphazardly. None of this is right, my hackles rising equal to my building concern.

"Everette..?" I keep my voice soft and placating, not knowing what the fuck is happening. I've never seen him like this. Even at the sound, my obvious approach, he doesn't stop. He doesn't even look at me. "Everette. Hey. What's going on? Talk to me." I surge the tiniest bit of a bark into my words. Not that it'll do much to another alpha, but it should do enough to get his attention, to make sure he hears me.

Head snapping up, his bright green eyes meet my golden ones, dark circles under them. My concern is overwhelming, inching towards him. I don't know what's got him so stressed, though, so I stay back a bit, not touching him or hugging him yet. I nod, smiling, and wait for a verbal acknowledgment.

His words come out gravely, as if he hasn't spoken. I realize quickly, he probably hasn't. "Hey, man." Clearing his throat a bit, his hands fall from his hair, the messy curls not entirely bouncing back into place, looking far more wild than usual.

"Are you okay? I wasn't expecting you back yet. Did...did something happen?"

He huffs, shaking his head as if in disbelief, continuing to pace back and forth a few feet. "Yes and no, I guess. Fuck, I don't know, honestly." His arms go wide, slapping against his sides, as he laughs forcefully. There's no humor in it. "The first couple of days were fine. Quiet, productive. Exactly what I was hoping to gain. And then... I don't know what happened. It was like I suddenly couldn't breathe fully, anxiety crawling under my skin, I couldn't sleep well... It was like a rock was forming under my skin, on my chest, growing heavier each day. I can't explain it. I just had to come home early. I knew... I mean, I knew logically that you all were okay; otherwise, the management team would have told me. But, fuck man. I had to come back, had to. Had to see for myself everything was okay. Fuck the retreat, ya know?"

He looks back up towards me, and I see tears lining his eyes, torment clear in every etch of his face as they threaten to fall. As his lead, I'm done waiting, done keeping a safe distance. He needs me, and I need to calm and protect him. Even if it is from himself and whatever demons he's fighting in that brain of his. Although, instinct is telling me exactly what's happening, and he's about to have his world flipped.

Ready for his alpha's wrath, tensed to fight, I step forward, moving to wrap my arms around him.

Closing the space between us eagerly, I feel the change in him. The exact moment the scent of our omega that lingered on my skin, my lips, my shirt from earlier this morning, hits him.

There is no doubt, she is Ever's scent match, too. All four of us are, as I expected.

Near-feral eyes, a few inches south of mine, fly to meet my gaze, narrowing. The most vicious snarl I'd ever heard from our calm, centered, loving alpha, shakes the room as his hands fist my shirt, pushing me back into the wall in desperation.

I could have stopped him, was ready for it, but I let his primal have this moment to expel the chaos eating him. Because *this* isn't Ever in front of me, it's his primal.

Seconds pass as we stare at each other, his eyes taking on an almost pleading quality under the feral beast that rides him hard. Bracing my feet, I grip his hands, ready for a fight, and simply nod, giving him the confirmation he needs for what he already knows.

Sharply releasing me, he pulls back, head whipping in the direction of the stairs and back to the front door. A constant vibration of his possessive growl reaches the corners of the large room as he lifts his head trying to scent Opaline on the air. In huffs of frustration, he tries to follow her nonexistent trail, coming up empty, only building his ire.

The look of feral determination in his eyes is undeniable as he stalks towards the door.

Our omega is about to meet her final alpha.

With those eyes more wild than I've ever seen them, Everette snarls, *"Where is she?"*

Thank you, dear reader...

The End.

Thank you SO much for reading and I hope you enjoyed Book One/Part One of the Knot Just A Wish Trilogy!

(Read ahead** for a sneak peek chapter of **Knot Just A Wish: Book Two!)

Book Two is out now!

Book Three is estimated to release September 2026!

I'd love to share the rest of Opaline and her Alphas' story through to their very happily ever after with you. Book One does a lovely job of setting up the rest of their story.

Also, if you enjoyed this book it would mean so much to me if you could leave even a quick review! Reviews are tremendously important to growing authors and I am genuinely appreciative for each and every single one. <3

Feel free to join me on Instagram and TikTok, too. I'd love to be friends!

@Author_Maren_Marlowe

Website:

authormarenmarlowe.com

About the author

First, thank you so much for being here and making it this far into the book!

Reading had become my escape when there was genuinely nothing left to keep me going. It allowed me to feel and experience a range of emotions I otherwise wouldn't have been able to. And then, I rediscovered true passion... in writing. When I was a young girl, my home life wasn't ideal. I would come home from school and isolate, writing stories and books. If only I knew then that I would be in my thirties, falling back in love with writing, and officially published!

Life can be incredibly difficult at times, and I think many readers tend to turn to books as a form of escapism.

Knowing that one of the books I publish might become someone's safe space or comfort-read makes all my late nights worth it, and then some. At the end of the day, that's my dream.

In each of my novels, I guarantee at least one truth of my own life and personal experience lives behind one or more of my MCs. Telling my story behind a mask and an entourage of fictional characters has been healing, and I hope that extends to the divine feminine everywhere.

Now the fun stuff!

I currently/temporarily live in the Midwest. Colorado will always feel like home. The mountains are healing (I swear by this! Haha). I'm working to be able to move back out West... hopefully all the way to the coast this time.

I work in tech as a CRM Systems & Database Administrator during the day at a Science Museum. As soon as I come home, I dive back into writing for several hours and then lie in bed doing word searches or reading until I fall asleep! I'm exciting like that.

My debut novel was a Dark-ish Romance that took me two years from start to finish. While I did have fun with it and have the next two plotted out... Omegaverse and why-choose is where my heart truly lives and where I will be spending my focus going forward!

Thank you so much for visiting Mountain Glow Hot Springs Resort ;)

It's here waiting whenever you need a little escape.

Also by the Author...

<u>Omegaverse</u>

Mount Fir's Landing

Mountain Glow Hot Springs Resort Series:

Knot Just A Wish: Book One

Knot Just A Wish: Book Two

Knot Just A Wish: Book Three

<u>Dark Romance</u>

Shadows Series:

No longer in print

<u>Coming Soon!</u>

Curious what sparks are between Beckett and Alina? Be on the look out for their story, coming soon!

A stand-alone contemporary why-choose is also in the works! Violet finds herself on a wintery getaway when her friend suddenly can't go, taking her place. Even better? The three mountain men that live in the prestigious ski town are desperate to show her just how wonderful having more than one boyfriend can really be... coming soon!

Part Two Sneak peek ahead...

CONTAINS SMALL SPOILERS

Please note there are brief, small spoilers in the bonus chapter ahead! If you want to be completely surprised going into Part Two, I would recommend stopping here.

This chapter is towards the middle of book two and was chosen specifically as a way to provide a teaser into certain character's growth as well as growing tension between packmates. With that little disclaimer, enjoy!

Knot Just A Wish: Book Two

CHAPTER 44

"What's going on with you two? I thought things were starting to, you know...level out?" Lottie asks with a curious stare.

"I thought so too. I really did. I mean, it was! But...with the way he looked at me tonight with utter disgust and disapproval..." I trail off a bit weakly. "I'm too scared to think about what it means for our supposed friendship." And the dynamic within our pack.

"Which is BS, by the way."

"What is? What do you mean?"

"I mean the fact that he's your fucking scent match!" Her outrage reverberates in the small space, even over the music pumping through hidden speakers, gathering attention from a couple of women at the bathroom's vanity. "Shit," she hisses, apologetically. "Sorry. It just upsets me. I can't imagine being in your shoes. You're handling it really well." Pushing off the tiled wall and turning fully, she gives me a quick hug, teetering slightly.

"There's nothing I can do about it. I just need to respect his boundaries and pathetically, take whatever he offers me." She shakes her head and crosses her arms. Internally, I agree and continue, "I know...but, honestly having bonded Calder, and having told Sage I love him? And god, Everette is so kind and gentle. I'm so thankful for them and each of our relationships. Seriously. This was already a happy ending I gave up on. So, the fact one of my *four* scent matches just wants to be friends? How can I really be angry?" I softly smile, Calder's love evident even now, through our bond. I mostly mean what I said. I want to fully mean it, I just wasn't quite there yet. Albeit, it is a little embarrassing to be pining over someone that really doesn't want me, so I keep it at that. Despite the fact that she's really the only person I can talk to about Adrian, I want to stop the conversation. I just started feeling better after his unexpected arrival here tonight.

Making our way back to the bar, we do what we absolutely should not: order shots. My gaze catches an angry Adrian in the huge expanse of glass behind the bar. I look away a little too quickly to be casual. It's a little unbelievable to me that Adrian actually has friends outside of Calder, Ever, and Sage. I guess I just must be the only one who gets this extra sweet version of him. Standing at the bar, we smile and shimmy happily as Tommy serves us something pale pink with one of his signature winks. I can say that now, since I've known him for over three hours.

"Cheers, babes! I'm having the best time!"

"Cheers!"

Raising the tiny glasses to our lips, we manage to take them in one go. It's surprisingly sweet and easy to shoot. Everything had started feeling a little heavier as the night progressed, but I'm having way too much fun to care anymore.

The sudden warmth and firm hold of a strong hand gripping my bicep gathers my startled attention, head whipping up. "Opaline, should you seriously be doing another shot? I think you're done," Adrian practically growls, eyes intense as he stares down at me.

The momentary shock I feel at him even acknowledging me slips away quickly, replaced with a small spark of anger that even surprises me a little with its ferocity. "Now you..." I try and fail to pull my arm out of his steel grip, "...want to talk to me? I'm fine and not your problem." He releases me, finally, eyes narrowed. I'm not scared of him anymore. Not like I was when we first met.

"Fine," he sneers.

"Fiiinnee," I echo, trying to clumsily push past him. "I'm going to go dance and have a wonderful evening, in fact," I say primly, chin in the air.

"Great."

"Great!" I'm starting to sound like a parrot even to my own ears. The image of me in a parrot costume flapping my wings like flamboyant pointed fingers towards this alphahole enters my mind and I vibrate with goofy laughter, stepping towards the dancefloor. Lottie's immediately at my side.

"That was so awesome!" she whispers next to my ear.

I laugh, leaning on her, my inner omega loving her freely cuddly nature. "Where are the others?"

"Probably just on the patio, they're fine. Come on!"

We make our way into the small crowd of people moving and dancing around us. A hip-hop, dance remix pumps through the air, the occasional sweaty arm or shoulder bumping us here and there. We sing along to the lyrics as they come, colored lights bouncing off Lottie's beautiful face and flushed cheeks, putting a spotlight on her perfect smile.

"Hey, pretty lady...look at you." A man, close enough to our age, with light brown hair comes up to our side seemingly out of nowhere, his breath strong of whiskey as he tries to lean in.

"I'm taken," I start, pulling my sweaty hair back to show off my healing bite mark. He tries to lean in again and I pull away before he can touch me, which seems to make him only want to try harder.

"Bite doesn't mean shit, hun. If he really wanted you, he'd be here. I've been watching you girls. A fresh bite like that?" He laughs. "He wanted you, he'd be here snarlin' at anyone so much as *looked* at you. I think your picker's wrong there, girl."

Logically, I know he's wrong. I *know* he is wrong, but, for some reason I still have a very real, visceral reaction to his words. It feels like it triggers something in me that had numbed from the alcohol. I can feel it start to take up residence in my body, unwelcomed. "I'm not interested," I say, but, it comes out weaker than I intend it to. He seems to notice, a wolfish grin stretching his lips that leaves an immediate sense of alarm in my chest.

"She said she's not interested!" Lottie bumps the guy, trying to get him out of our space and go back to dancing, but, I know it won't be that easy. I hate to admit, but this might be a good time to have Adrian keeping watch. Glancing at the bar hoping to make eye contact, my brows furrow. He isn't there? He'd been in the same spot all night...

"Yeah, and I'm not talkin' to you, wannabe omega." Turning his attention forcefully back to me, his fingertips just barely land on my hips before a huge blur of black appears out of nowhere, slamming the guy against the closest wall. I gasp, nearly losing my balance. Fuck, maybe that last shot really was a bad idea.

"Adrian!" I yell, Lottie gripping my arm, steadying me. Beckett, I realize had come to our side too, near his sister. He glances at Lottie with concern before his attention turns back to Adrian with a shit-eating grin. His presence is a relief I didn't know I needed. Adrian is fucking terrifying right now. I'm not scared of him for myself, I know now that he would genuinely never hurt me. But, anyone else, like this guy he currently has pinned against the wall by the neck with his forearm? I'm really not so sure he'll be leaving with his face still in tact. I manage to step a little closer, trying to get his attention, to make him stop.

"Put your hands on my fucking omega again and we'll see if your legs still work long enough to walk out." The man looks like he's suddenly much more sober than a minute ago, sputtering and pressing against his arm to try to get free from his unyielding grasp. *"Got it?"* He somehow manages to nod before Adrian releases him and I realize he's on his tip-toes, being held up.

There's a small crowd of people eyeing the scene warily, now. I know Tommy or security will be here soon.

Despite the scene in front of me, his words ring through me again...and again.

My omega.

Acknowledgements

Finally...

Thank you to Joanie, my closest friend.

Without a family or support system, you have been the one person in my life I can always count on.

You are my biggest cheerleader when it comes to pursuing my dreams of being an Author. You've been by my side through the long days and nights, the stress, the doubt, tears, and now, the celebrations.

I'm not sure you will ever know the extent of my gratitude and the love and admiration I hold for you.

The kindest person in this world and somehow my best friend.

I am so blessed.

Thank you.

www.ingramcontent.com/pod-product-compliance
Lightning Source LLC
LaVergne TN
LVHW100520110826
845146LV00002B/718
9798994381915